POSTCARDS FROM THE SEASIDE

LAURIE HORNSBY

APS BOOKS
YORKSHIRE

APS Books,
The Stables, Field Lane,
Aberford,
West Yorkshire,
LS25 3AE

APS Books is a subsidiary of
the APS Publications imprint

www.andrewsparke.com

CHAPTER 1

TO WHERE THE BRASS BAND PLAYS TIDDLY UM POM POM

'You will address all correspondence to Mister Lester Duvall, care of the Brighton Hippodrome!' was the rude and abrupt response from an agitated passenger to the elderly ticket collector whose only crime had been to politely ask 'May I see your ticket sir?'

With the train shuddering to a screeching halt this ill mannered and impatient passenger then easily brushed the frail gentleman aside to swiftly alight from the buffet carriage and down onto the platform where, as if by magic, he vanished into the swirling mist of engine steam.

Clad in a grey gabardine raincoat, small suitcase in hand and with head held high, Mister Lester Duvall, gentleman of the theatre, then strode confidently through the station's booking hall and out into the early evening air of late May 1940.

There were no taxi cabs to be hailed. Petrol rationing had seen to that. Not that it made the slightest difference. His pocket did not run to such luxury.

Guided by the distant sound of squawking gulls and the salty smell of the sea, within fifteen minutes Mister Duvall was strutting along the clifftop path that hovered above the town's harbour. The sight of small boats bobbing around in their moorings proved impossible to resist and he therefore paused for a minute or two to take in the view.

Members of a brass band, having performed an afternoon concert at the harbour entrance, could be seen loading their various instruments onto a couple of hand carts whilst a cockles and whelks trader was hoovering up any passing trade there was to be had. Four weary donkeys, following a day long stint on the sands, were being urged on by their cane waving master, a little old chap of dilatory appearance, to go clipperty clopping their way along the happy trails of the promenade.

Opposite the harbour entrance, in all its grandeur, stood the Royal Hotel but Mister Duvall immediately came to the conclusion that its tariff would be way out of his league.

Without any thought as to what would be his destiny, shading his eyes he gazed out across the English Channel to beyond the blue horizon. Obviously the problems British troops were currently encountering on the beaches of Dunkirk had been the main topic of conversation among fellow passengers during his train journey but Mister Lester Duvall had far more important things to concern himself with.

The bill poster on the outside wall of a tiny fleapit theatre eased his apprehension. It read 'Postcards from the Seaside starring the Topsy Turvys and Mister Lester Duvall'. At least he was expected.

To the side of this dilapidated, weather bashed shack of a place was a door on which had been haphazardly daubed, in white paint, the words 'Stage Door'. Easing open the creaking door Mister Duvall found himself entering warily into a strange world of fusty semi-dark eeriness.

'We'd more or less give up on you,' came a half-whispered voice from between the bedraggled shabby curtains that were in fact the stage wings. The voice then revealed itself to be that of a middle aged gent, lacking in height and hair and wearing a frayed at the lapels old black dinner suit.

Climbing the four wooden steps up to stage level, Mister Duvall, offering an introductory hand, attempted to enquire about possible overnight accommodation but was immediately overridden by the whispering gent.

'The Topsys will do about ten minutes and then it's over to you, oh and you're in number two dressing room,' he added, pointing to a door upon which a brass number hung loosely and hopelessly askew.

Miming a 'thank you' Mister Duvall turned to make for his appointed dressing room but the gent took a hold of his arm.

'If you can stick in a bit o' spiel about our lads over at Dunkirk you might do yerself a bit o' good,' whispered the gent, winking cheekily.

The striking up of a hopelessly out of tune piano then cued the whispering gent to religiously cross himself before venturing out into the limelight where he proclaimed to all seated in front of him, 'Welcome to the opening night of our fun-filled variety show *Postcards From the Seaside!* And believe me you're welcome to it!'

Without making eye contact two feminine little cuties, dressed in identical Pierrot clown outfits, came scurrying past but, unperturbed, Mister Duvall made for his appointed dressing room where, upon entry, he was near startled to death by a sudden announcement from a wall-mounted loudspeaker.

'Ladies and gentlemen,' the speaker cackled, 'I give you The Topsy Turvys!'

On tiptoe, with an arm at full stretch, Mister Duvall's eager fingers sought the wire that was, as expected, soldered to the back of the cobwebbed and dusty old speaker cone and with one short sharp jerk the annoying contraption was silenced once and for all.

Placing his small suitcase on the collapsible table in the middle of the room the gentleman of the theatre removed his raincoat to sling it casually onto a wicker chair placed in the corner of the room. However, with the chair legs proving decidedly wobbly a nail on the back of the door immediately became the preferred choice for the raincoat. Flicking open his case Mister Duvall quickly removed its contents, a straw boater hat and a candy-striped blazer, both of which would prove the ideal combination for the shiny at the rear black flannel trousers he was already wearing. Just like the flannels, the blazer had seen far better days whilst the shirt and shoes would be the same ones he'd had on all day, the day before and the day before that. Producing a little black dickie bow from the top pocket of the blazer, Mister Duvall, fastening and then concealing the tie beneath the collar of his shirt, popped himself into the blazer. The icing on the cake would be the straw boater.

By utilising the full length heavily cracked mirror that leant precariously against a flaking wall, the gentleman of the theatre patted his black hair down flat to juggle with the boater until its brim hung cheekily over the brow of his forehead. A warm up routine consisting of a ten second soft shoe shuffle, complete with a 360-degree swivel, would be concluded by an on the beat clap of his shimmering hands for good measure.

The suggestion made by the middle-aged gent in regard to a 'bit of spiel' was beginning to make sense to him and so, moving with haste from his dressing room, up the wooden steps to await introduction, Mister Lester Duvall found himself mentally sketching out some form of an emotional speech whilst clumsily hopping from one leg to the other, rubbing his shoes up and down the back of his trousers in an effort to revive any previous shine that might have once existed.

Reducing their audience to a state of uncontrollable laughter, the Topsy Turvys now chose to break the flow of their cornball patter with a well rehearsed but way over the top syrupy introduction.

'Ladies and gentlemen,' they both hollered in perfect unison, 'we are delighted to introduce to you a gentleman you've probably heard singing on the wireless with Billy Cotton!' causing an impressive gasp from the not too sparse audience to flutter around the dank auditorium. Obviously the promotional letter, sent in advance by Mister Duvall, telling of a highly distinguished show business career had not gone unread.

'This gentleman should have been spending his summer at the Brighton Hippodrome in the company of Max Miller!' they exclaimed, inducing the audience to the edge of their seats. 'But due to the threat of flying visits from Herr Adolph Hitler, the Brighton Hippodrome has been forced to close its doors for the foreseeable future.'

Although sympathetic sighs resounded around the theatre, help was at hand to revive the fledging spirit.

'But Brighton's loss is our gain!' the Topsy Turvys joyously proclaimed. 'He's here, with us, on the Isle of Thanet, for the entire summer season! Ladies and gentlemen, we give you Mister Lester Duvall!'

Arms fully outstretched and wearing the broadest of grins Mister Lester Duvall, gentleman of the theatre, bounded onstage to make the most confident of entrances. Bowing to acknowledge his audience before taking a Topsy Turvy on each arm, he then proceeded to glide the two little ladies gracefully around the stage whilst singing the most apt of lyric.

'He sends her postcards from the seaside. Warm greetings and beside
Crossed kisses he wishes she were there.'
He'd take her promenading, then be serenading
Her on the swing boats at the fair.

All those kisses he'd be stealing would send her heart a reeling
As the brass band played oompah on the pier
Postcards from the seaside, warm greetings and beside,'

Waving his straw boater high in the air, with the Topsy Turvys moving in closer, the gentleman of the theatre brought the song to a dramatic conclusion with unceasing gusto.

'Postcards from the seaside, wish you were here!'

Basking in the rapturous applause, Lester Duvall paused briefly to gesture for calm before delivering his newly concocted piece of dialogue in the most somber of manner.

'Ladies and gentlemen I'm sure there is no need to remind you that, as I speak, stranded on the beaches of Dunkirk, just twenty odd miles or so across the English Channel, are our boys, our boys, ladies and gentlemen, preparing themselves to take on the might of the German army.'

With the theatre falling into a deeply respectful silence, sensing the audience were putty in his hands, and in keeping with his nature, the gentleman of the theatre went for broke.

'Our boys, fighting like lions for their King and country,' he stated, raising a clenched fist. 'Let us pray for their safe return. Indeed let us vow to bring the boys home soon.'

If the folks were looking for some kind of a morale booster then they had certainly found one.

With the pianist vamping a stirring marching rhythm the Topsy Turvys began to move militarily either side of Mister Duvall as he, seemingly from the heart, sang out his patriotic and highly emotional plea.

Let's bring the boys home soon. Let's hope the next full moon
Sees all the fighting done with Gerry on the run
And Hitler sinking faster than a lead balloon

Home fires will always burn until their safe return
Boys so boldly brave they risk an early grave, marching to
our nation's tune.
Into the fires of Hell, God bless and keep them well
Let's bring the boys home soon!

It would be fair to say that the reaction to his song could only be have been matched by the second coming of the Messiah.

At a small rickety table adjacent to the stage door sat the middle aged gent, shaking his head in bewilderment as he endeavoured to pencil the evening's box office figures into a little red notebook.

'Sorry to disturb but I didn't catch your name earlier,' said Mister Duvall as he approached.

Now minus the ash stained monkey jacket, dickie bow and studded collar, the middle aged gent, popped the notebook down into his trouser pocket. Bringing himself to his feet he formally introduced himself.

'I'm Sid, emcee, stage door and general dogs round 'ere,' he stated with a voice of authority. 'But first may I say sir what a pleasure it is to be workin' with a true gentleman o' the featre like your good self,' before adding 'an' if I was wearin' me titfer *(Tit for tat/hat)* I'd take it orf to yer.'

However, seeking to respond to these compliments Mister Duvall found himself on the receiving end of a gentle nudge in the ribs from Sid.

'That bit you done about our lads over there, it was just what the doctor ordered,' he said, wryly winking his eye before moving on to a rather more pressing matter.

'Now regardin' digs for yerself, I reckon your best bet is Gerty Skidmore. She's just across the road in Waterloo

Street, number 65. It's one of the 'ouses what faces the Spotted Dog pub. Gerty serves up a good breakfast, there's plenty of it and it don't arrive too early,' Sid stated in a manner that suggested the establishment to be the working man's equivalent of the Ritz.

'And would that be a Mrs or a Miss Skidmore?' Mister Duvall nosily inquired.

Raising his index finger to indicate confidentiality, Sid, in a crafty half whisper, spelled out Gerty's personal predicament as it presently stood.

'The ol' man ain't around at the moment on account of 'im runnin' orf with the barmaid from the Spotted Dog. But you ain't 'eard that from me, alright?'

Mister Duvall nodded his head. Confidentiality at all times would be adhered to.

Robustly opening the stage door Sid then stepped out onto the cliff top pathway followed by Mister Duvall who couldn't help but notice that the poor chap walked with a not too prominent a limp but, being the gentleman that he was, he chose not to comment.

'Blimey, it's a bit nippy round the orchestras *(Orchestra stalls/balls)* tonight,' Sid chuckled, briskly rubbing his hands together. 'Follow the footpath down there, 'ang a right at the bandstand, cross over the road and you're lookin' at Waterloo Street. Got it?' he stated but it would be Mister Duvall's look of total bewilderment that caused Sid to impatiently reiterate.

'Listen, down to the bandstand, 'ang a right an' Waterloo Street is right in front o' yer. Number 65 is one o' the 'ouses what faces the Spotted Dog. Do yerself a favour an' tell Gerty I sent yer!' That was Sid's parting shot before returning into the much needed warmth of the theatre, not forgetting to slam the stage door firmly behind him.

CHAPTER 2

DON'T DILLY DALLY ON THE WAY

Out on the pathway the only sound to be heard was that of the roaring of the sea crashing wildly onto the shingled beach some sixty feet below. Tucking his head down into the upturned collar of his raincoat Mister Duvall crossed his fingers and set off in the direction that Sid had indicated. As instructed, at the bandstand he veered to his right and skirting a heap of stacked deckchairs he crossed the road to where, lo and behold, Waterloo Street awaited. Entering the street he found his arrival heralded by the plaintiff cries of a pub landlord pleading with his customers to 'see these drinks orf please!'

The open door of the Spotted Dog revealed a saloon bar and, through the haze of tobacco smoke, Mister Duvall was able to observe a room pretty full of well-lubricated men, many of whom, despite the lateness of the hour, were still clad in grubby working clothes.

Directly opposite the pub, just as Sid had said, stood a row of half a dozen or so modestly-sized three-storey Victorian terraced houses, one of which bore the number 65 on its front door and would require four steps up from the pavement in order to reach its knocker.

Mister Duvall's initial rather flimsy tap met with no response.

A second and more firm attempt proved successful.

'Who is it?' a woman's voice inquired faintly from within.

He called back to her, 'Hello, is that Mrs Skidmore?'

'Who wants to know?' asked the voice, this time in a more demanding tone.

'Mrs Skidmore, my name is Lester Duvall and I'm led to believe by Sid the stage doorman that you take in gentlemen of the theatre.'

Very slowly the door began to open and, seizing upon the opportunity, Mister Duvall endeavoured to pick up from where he'd left off. 'Mrs Skidmore I'm with the Postcards…' only for him to be silenced in mid flight.

'You'd better come in then,' stated the woman, opening the door fully.

In her mid-thirties, her black curled hair more or less concealed beneath a flowery turban and wearing a pinafore that begged for tomorrow to be wash day, Gerty Skidmore looked and sounded a typical 1940's seaside landlady.

Leading the gentleman into her kitchen, a room illuminated by two candles, both in saucers at either end of a sideboard and kept upright by lumps of congealed wax, Mister Duvall attempted further introduction.

'Mrs Skidmore I do realise this is rather short notice for you,' he said. 'I should have been at the Brighton Hippodrome with Max Miller but…'

'You'll be the bloke with the Topsy Turvys then?' she again interrupted. 'You can't be too careful with this war on.'

'And they said it would all be over by Christmas,' he wistfully commented. 'Well, here we are, into May and…'

'I was listenin' to the news earlier on the wireless,' said Gerty, picking up a half bottle of gin from the table. 'Our boys are 'avin' it a bit rough over in France. Still it might make a difference now Chamberlain's out the way. Winston will get it sorted,' she added with an air of confidence.

'And you are absolutely right,' agreed Mister Duvall, not wishing to ruffle any feathers. 'Like you Mrs Skidmore I have complete and utter faith in Mister Churchill's abilities.'

'So 'ow long you 'ere for then?' Gerty asked, pouring a good measure of neat gin into her tea cup to then aim the rim of the bottle at a spare cup. 'Fancy a drop?' she asked invitingly but Mister Duvall, immediately covering the empty cup with the palm of his hand, went into panic mode.

'No thank you!' he snapped, indicating absolute sobriety. 'I never touch the stuff, and I never have! But to answer your question, going by tonight's performance, I would imagine I will be here until mid September at least. The Topsy Turvys are two very funny little ladies.'

'About as funny as a wooden leg if you're askin' me?' said an unimpressed Gerty. Shrugging her shoulders, she downed her cup of gin with one fell swoop. 'They 'ad Max Miller up the road in Margate last summer, was you with 'im then?' she inquired, smacking her lips.

Mister Duvall shook his head. 'As I recall I was otherwise engaged,' was his aloof reply.

'You can 'ave the room, top o' the first flight o' stairs, the one on the left,' Gerty stated. 'It's a pound a week for bed, breakfast and supper, all of which includes full use o' the cruets,' she hiccuped, pouring herself yet another healthy measure of mother's ruin from the rapidly depleting bottle. 'Anyway, where's your suitcase?' she casually asked, wiping her lips on her pinafore.

'I left it back at the featre,' yawned Mister Duvall, patting his mouth with his hand.

'Featre, you said featre?' Gerty asked suspiciously. 'You ain't from down the Ol' Kent Road way are yer?'

'Deary me no!' the gentleman answered in true upper lip fashion. 'My family roots lie a little more to the north and some way over to the east. Are you by any chance familiar with Constable?' he enquired.

'I've been to Dunstable,' replied a bewildered Gerty before reeling off the general rules of the house. Breakfast would be at ten and served in the kitchen. Supper, always bread and pickles, would be served in his room either before or after his performance, the choice would be his. Finally Gerty delivered the golden rule that was to be adhered to at all times.

'No fancy women in yer room!' she roared, pointing a finger at him. 'There'll be no 'anky panky in my 'ouse!'

'Mrs Skidmore I happen to be a gentleman of the theatre,' spluttered an astonished Mister Duvall. 'And I consider such comments to be a slight on my good character.'

'Good!' snapped Gerty. 'You'll find a pot under the bed. For solids it's always the privy up the top o' the yard.'

Lifting a saucer that contained one of the lit candles off the sideboard Gerty handed it to Mister Duvall. 'You'd better take this to 'elp find your way up the stairs, and don't forget to douse the wick before you drop off.'

'Then I will bid you goodnight Mrs Skidmore,' bade Mister Duvall as with a candle to light his way, he ascended the stairs.

'And talkin' o' candles,' said Gerty, calling up to him from the foot of the staircase. 'If yer need the back yard privy, don't lean back or you'll singe yer 'air on the candle!'

Waking to the sound of squawking seagulls on that first morning but struggling to raise his head from the pillow Mister Duvall finally drew upon his inner strength and clambered out from beneath the wafer thin blanket. Pulling the shoddy curtains back to allow some light into the sparsely furnished room he noted a dining chair and a small table placed alongside a dust-caked single dark brown utility wardrobe, its door hanging more or less off the hinges. In the opposite corner of the room, adjacent to the window, stood a heavily scummed white wash basin that was playing host to the bone hard remnants of what had once been a bar of carbolic soap. Half in and half out of the well, a shaving razor, its blade heavily clogged with the whiskers of previous guests, was readily available for his use whilst a small oval mirror, peppered over the years by the flickings of carbolic soap, hung precariously from a nail maybe eighteen inches or so above the basin.

Upon the wooden rail, positioned on the wall alongside the basin, having arrived mysteriously during the night, was a clean hand towel, but it would be the smell of frying eggs and bacon wafting up the staircase that willed Mister Duvall to find the courage to swish the cold tap water vigorously in the direction of his face. A rather wild slobbering into the towel resulted in the conclusion that life was good. And so, as he was about to discover, was his breakfast.

'Nothing short of par excellence Mrs Skidmore!' he chuckled, patting his stomach to indicate satisfaction. 'I could have eaten a horse and chased the driver! Yes indeed, I do have an awful lot to thank Sid for,' he sighed, mopping a final slice of heavily buttered bread around his plate

'E's got 'is reasons, the randy ol' barsket,' sneered Gerty, putting the record straight. 'All Sid wants is to get 'is boots under my bed! And talkin' o' beds,' she snapped, 'the rent is a week in advance,' before adding sarcastically 'that is if you don't mind.'

Utilising his tongue to prise a smattering of congealed egg yolk from the corner of his mouth Mister Lester Duvall, gentleman of the theatre, made his plea for mercy.

'Mrs Skidmore I'm afraid my train fare proved a little more than I envisaged,' he uttered in a voice that quivered with emotion. 'I've also been forced to lay out a fair few pennies on a striped blazer and straw boater, all of which has rendered me, for the time being anyway, financially embarrassed.'

A glass eye would have received more sympathy. 'So what's a straw boater got to do with the price o' taters then?' Gerty acidly queried as she began clearing the table of crockery and his elbows.

'You see, as I finish my song 'Postcards from the Seaside', I wave the straw boater at the audience,' Mister Duvall nervously replied.

The silence was deafening.

Drawing heavily on his thespian skills, in a last pitch to conjure sympathy, Mister Duvall played the only card available to him. 'I suppose I could have a word with the Topsy Turvys about an advance on my wages,' he sighed, crossing his fingers beneath the table.

'Nah, leave it, I'll manage,' she replied, taking the sting out of the rather tense atmosphere. 'I 'spose you'll need a front door key.'

With Gerty rummaging in the top drawer of her sideboard Mister Lester Duvall gazed upwards to offer silent thanks to the Almighty.

'I promised I'd pull the pints over the Spotted Dog this mornin'. My ol' man's 'opped it with the barmaid, but I 'spose Sid's told you that already,' Gerty mumbled, continuing to mooch.

Sussing that a diversion from such a delicate subject was called for, Mister Duvall arose from the breakfast table to announce that '...following my morning perambulation the rest of the day will find me at the theatre, rehearsing my routine.'

The diversion had worked beautifully.

'Say 'ello to Sid for me, oh and remind him I'm comin' to the show tonight,' Gerty said, handing him a door key. 'The Topsy Turvys always invite us landladies along to their second night.'

Heading for the door Mister Duvall innocently inquired. 'And I presume you then recommend our show to your holiday making guests?'

'What guests?' Gerty mused. 'Ain't nobody told you there's a war on?

Like everything else Mrs Skidmore's response went flying over the fancy free head of Mister Lester Duvall and so, with the most carefree of attitude, he skipped merrily down the front four steps of number 65 to land upon the sun-kissed pavement where he commenced his morning constitutional.

Leaving Waterloo Street behind, crossing the road, as his pace developed into a brisk march, the gentleman of the theatre was soon whistling out his well stocked repertoire for the pleasure of anyone who cared to listen. Waltzing around the same two hand carts that had been parked at the harbour entrance the previous early evening, a casual glance to the bandstand confirmed that, with various members of the brass band setting down their music stands, an afternoon concert was definitely on the cards.

Above him the gulls were gliding high and mightily on the chilly breeze, celebrating the fact that the month of June was merely a heartbeat away.

Indeed Mister Duvall was himself aware of that very same chill but remained confident that as spring became summer the days would grow longer and warmer.

Slowing his pace to a leisurely stroll he peered into the distance and beheld his place of work. To say that this palace of variety stood majestically on the cliff tops would be gross exaggeration but its purpose was to generate fun and happiness for all who ventured inside and, on that point alone, the place most definitely did succeed.

Being a single man of a certain age, in his case, like his new landlady, mid-thirties, Mister Duvall's plan of action had always been to hone in on the fine middle class type of lady, the type who would be game for a brief holiday romance whilst picking up the tabs on his behalf. This philosophy having served him well over the course of his illustrious career the gentleman of the theatre saw no reason whatsoever to change a winning formula.

Squinting in the bright sunlight he observed activity around the stage door and, drawing closer, ascertained that it was Sid, complete with brush and paste bucket, attempting, without much success, to secure a promotional poster onto the outside wall of the theatre.

The usual 'How were the digs, how was the breakfast?' chit chat ping ponged between the two men until Mister Duvall reminded Sid that Mrs Skidmore would be in attendance that very evening. 'Oh and I nearly forgot,' he added, 'Gerty said to say hello.'

Despairingly Sid plonked his brush down into the paste bucket. 'Just 'ello then was it?' he sighed with more than an air of disappointment. 'Oh well, I've got me artistes to think about. They don't give me 'alf a crown a week for nothin'.

'Half a crown a week?' asked a slightly confused Mister Duvall. 'Why should anyone give you half a crown a week?'

Bringing himself to an upright stance Sid was in no mood to take prisoners. 'It is featrical tradition sir,' he snapped. 'Blokes like me 'ave to be rewarded for what they do on be'alf o' blokes like you!'

'You mean you expect me to give you half a crown?' Mister Duvall gasped in disbelief.

'That is quite correct sir, every week, and in advance,' Sid confirmed, holding out his right hand in anticipation. 'It can be a long cold winter round this neck o' the woods.'

Never one to mince his words a thoroughly displeased Mister Duvall let it be known that having paid Mrs Skidmore a week's rent in advance his financial standing, for the time being, was that of a man not in possession of the proverbial pot.

Cool as a cucumber Sid reached into the breast pocket of his grubby brown cow gown to produce the very same small red notebook that contained the theatre's financial audits.

'Don't worry sir, I'll just make a note in my little book,' said Sid craftily, dabbing the tip of a tiny pencil on his tongue, slowly mumbling the actual words that he was scrawling into his little red notebook.

'Mister Lester Duvall owes me one week,' he sighed, returning the notebook and pencil to his breast pocket before offering sound advice to his newly acquired client.

'You just keep yourself on the move and they'll never nail yer,' whispered Sid from out the side of his mouth, winking at Mister Duvall as he did so.

But this cloak and dagger sarcasm made Mister Duvall uncomfortable enough to warily ask 'Who won't, as you so quaintly put it, nail me?'

'The blokes in aufority, them what serves the call up papers on unsuspectin' poor ol' souls like you,' chuckled Sid, raising his eyebrows teasingly. 'I'm a bit too old for all that caper, plus I got me wonky leg, but you're all over the place, one day Brighton, next day Isle o' Fanet and the next day, well who knows?'

Strangely for a performer of professional standing Mister Duvall was dumbstruck.

And then he saw her.

CHAPTER 3

IN CASE A CERTAIN LITTLE LADY PASSES BY

Wearing a flimsy, light brown cardigan hanging loosely over a white-laced blouse and a flowing grey-coloured skirt she came into his life.

Petite, blue eyes and aged late twenties, the little lady had a tiny summery straw hat perched upon a bun of blonde hair which rendered her femininely divine. In short she was everything a hot-blooded man could ever wish for and, what with being well versed in the art of wooing younger members of the female fraternity, Mister Lester Duvall, gentleman of the theatre, 'accidentally on purpose' bumped into her.

'Whoops! Oh I do beg your pardon!' he exclaimed as his arms quickly found their way around her middle. 'My fault entirely,' he added, bringing her trim body much closer in to his.

Flustered by the gentleman's familiarity whilst still in the grip of his arms, the young lady was struggling to return her tiny straw hat to its favoured position when Mister Duvall relaxed his hold and stepped back.

'Would you excuse me my dear?' he asked in a somewhat syrupy, sugary tone 'I have my routine to rehearse and I'm running rather late as it is. Perhaps I'll have the pleasure of bumping into you again sometime?' he said light heartedly as turning away from the lady he retreated, via the stage door, into the backstage area of the theatre.

In the darkened silence he stood panting for breath in an effort to regain composure. He'd always taken advantage of the perks that came with his profession and there was little doubt about it, Mister Duvall had encountered a fair few classy ladies in his time, some of whom could be categorised as 'forbidden fruit' but past experience had taught him never to overplay his hand, especially at the 'getting to know you' stage. However, it soon dawned upon him that, in this case, the spanner in the works would be the little lady's age.

Previously he had always given preference to the more mature, lonely at heart type of woman, simply because they tended to be more sympathetic and consequently more gullible to his hard luck stories, but instinct was telling him that this encounter might turn out to be quite different from anything he'd experienced before.

Could it be the fragrance of the little lady's 'California Poppy' perfume that was driving him wild with desire? Who knows, but the fact remained that this little lady was awash with the stuff.

Outside the stage door, on the clifftop pathway, the young lady was in the process of rallying herself back to normality following her surprise encounter. Smoothing down her skirt and having made the appropriate adjustments to the position of the summery hat upon her head the little lady couldn't help but notice the promotional poster that Sid was doing his best to paste onto the wall. Unwittingly she began to read out the wording on the poster to herself.

'Postcards from the seaside, a variety show starring the Topsy Turvys and Mister Lester Duvall. Duvall? Lester Duvall?' the lady muttered to herself as a bell began to ring inside her pretty little head.

'Can I 'elp you madam?' asked Sid, carefully manoeuvring his paste bucket from around her feet, trying his utmost to avoid splashing any of the sloppy stuff over her sensible shoes.

'That gentleman who was just here, would he be a Topsy Turvy?' she innocently inquired, causing Sid to guffaw loudly.

'Who 'im, nah,' laughed Sid. 'That gentleman is Mister Lester Duvall!'

'But I'm sure I've heard the name Duvall somewhere before,' the lady replied, shaking her head in confusion. 'Has Mister Duvall ever performed on the wireless?' she asked.

'If I was to say to you the Billy Cotton show,' answered Sid, raising his eyebrows, causing the lady to gasp in amazement.

'You mean that gentleman, the one I've just encountered, has actually sung on the wireless with Billy Cotton!'

Before realizing what was happening, the star-struck little chickadee was being escorted by Sid through the stage door, up the four wooden steps and into the curtained wings where she would witness, first hand, the sight of Mister Lester Duvall putting himself through his paces.

'Don't worry, 'e owes me a favour anyway,' said Sid reassuringly, producing a chair for the lady's benefit. 'Sit yourself down 'ere an' I'll put the kettle on,' he added in a fatherly manner as suddenly the whole scenario sprang into life.

'Okay, we're going from the top!' Mister Duvall's voice boomed from the wings on the other side of the stage to then cue in the pianist by calling out 'Maestro, if you please, one two three and…'

In true Vaudeville style, with fingers popping on hands that were flapping, from the wings sprang the man himself. Soft shoe shuffling to centre stage and with his face bearing a fixed ear to ear grin, Mister Lester Duvall, gentleman of the theatre, launched into song.

'He sends her postcards from the seaside. Warm greetings and beside
Crossed kisses he wishes she were there.'

Seated in the wings, the little lady began patting her knees joyfully in time to the song's ragtime tempo as Mister Duvall gracefully swayed to the jazzy rhythm for in his mind he was sending thanks to the ecclesiastical powers above. His 'accidentally on purpose' ploy had not been in vain.

Finally, as the song resolved, so his empty arms reached out into the darkness to embrace his supposed audience. Silence abounded until the lady was unable to contain herself a moment longer.

Leaping to her feet she rushed to him. 'Bravo Mister Duvall!' she cried. 'Bravo!'

Being a gentleman of modest persuasion Lester Duvall acknowledged the praise with a simple smile.

'Madam you have the advantage,' he calmly stated, holding out an introductory hand.

'Oh but how silly of me, it's Miss Bagshaw, Miss Emily Bagshaw,' she giggled, grasping his hand to vigorously shake it.

'And where are you staying Miss Bagshaw?' he inquired. 'My money's on the Royal.'

'Nothing so grand I'm afraid, and I'd much prefer Emily,' she replied, feeling her inner self calming. 'I'm staying with my aunt for a few days, until Tuesday. My aunt is rather elderly and is, at present, extremely nervous.'

'What on earth has she got to be so nervous about?' asked a bewildered Mister Duvall.

'Haven't you heard the news?' Emily asked surprisingly. 'The wireless has been full of it all morning? Gerry is now positioned outside of Dunkirk and closing in rapidly, forcing Tommy to retreat onto the beaches.'

'And your aunt is concerned?' he sheepishly asked

'Concerned? The poor lady is quaking in her bed socks!' gasped Emily. 'My aunt is convinced that the German army will any day now sail into the harbour, goose-step up the promenade and shoot down anyone that cares to stand in their way.'

Needing to grab a lifeline quickly - after all there was a holiday romance at stake - Mister Duvall acted upon impulse and chose to inquire as to where her aunt resided.

'My aunt lives on Waterloo Street,' was Emily's reply. 'At Waterloo House to be precise.'

'Waterloo House?' asked a surprised Mister Duvall. 'Isn't that the baronial palace alongside the Spotted Dog?'

'Yes, unfortunately, my aunt's house is right next door to that dreadful place,' Miss Bagshaw answered, sounding none too pleased. 'Oh Mister Duvall, the language that spills from that establishment really is quite foul. The clientele of that public house is really the lowest of the low.'

'I use the place a lot as it 'appens,' muttered Sid approaching.

Juggling a tin tray laden with three full to the brim tea cups rattling around in their saucers Sid was somehow managing to balance the tray precariously on the top of the piano to then serve the morning's elevenses with nary a trace of eloquence.

'But I'm staying on Waterloo Street, with Mrs Skidmore, at number 65,' an excited Mister Duvall replied. 'We more or less face each other!'

Sadly the flow of conversation was disrupted as Sid clumsily attempted to return the spillage of tea from his saucer back into its cup, which led to Emily acting as if she hadn't noticed anything untoward at all.

Taking a pretend sip of her tea, her darting eyes searched here, there and everywhere for somewhere to discreetly place her cup and saucer without causing offence.

Unfortunately Mister Duvall had gulped down a good fifty per cent of his cup's content when his eyeballs suddenly shot up into his forehead. Fighting to contain the shock to his system the gentleman of the theatre shrieked 'Good Lord! This tea is awful!'

'That's it!' cried Emily, pointing at Mister Duvall in amazement. 'Lester Duvall! I knew I'd heard the name before! You and I were on the same train yesterday afternoon! You travelled the whole journey in the buffet car! And you almost choked on your tea then!'

'Hardly surprising,' spluttered Mister Duvall, sensing trouble. 'It was railway tea after all.'

'Oh no,' giggled Emily cheekily. 'It was when the elderly ticket collector chappy tapped you on the shoulder. I rather got the impression you were trying to dodge him.'

With colour draining from Mister Duvall's face, Emily, unaware of the embarrassment she was causing him, continued with the character assassination.

'You must remember! As the train came to a halt at the station you blurted out your name to the gentleman, Lester Duvall, care of the Brighton Hippodrome. Then, quick as a flash, you pushed the poor old fellow out of your way and jumped off the train!'

Forcing a grin onto his wincing face Mister Duvall quickly redirected the flow of their conversation with minimum disruption.

'So, have you anything planned for this evening, Emily?' he asked, praying that the events of that train journey would be consigned to the bowels of history.

'Well my aunt takes her cocoa in bed at 7 o'clock,' she answered. 'So I would imagine I will spend the rest of the evening alone with my knitting.'

Continuing down the path of politeness, Mister Duvall popped the obvious into the equation. 'Anything on the go at the moment?' he nonchalantly inquired.

'Only a balaclava for brother Bertie,' replied Emily.

'Well brother Bertie and his balaclava will have to wait,' Mister Duvall stated emphatically before asking Sid if it were possible to arrange a seat for Emily at the evening performance.

'That is what I'm 'ere for!' replied Sid, springing to attention. 'You just leave everything to Sidney.'

Emily nodded excitedly to confirm, thus setting the arrangement in stone before she bade her farewells to skip merrily away and clear out of sight.

However, as lustful thoughts returned to the mind of the love struck Romeo, so his rib cage received an unexpected and rather forceful nudge from Sid's elbow.

'A word in your ear if you don't mind sir?' asked Sid, tugging at Mister Duvall's jacket sleeve.

'Yes, yes!' answered Lester Duvall impatiently, waving into the darkness, hoping that he was still within Emily's sightings.

'What I need to know is, regardin' that young lady, are your intentions honourable or dishonourable?' asked Sid suspiciously

'You mean I get a choice?' replied Mister Duvall, massaging his ribs.

But Mister Duvall's flippancy was irritating Sid. 'You know full well I got lovin' feelin's for Gerty Skidmore,' he stated annoyingly. 'An' I've also got a little boat in the 'arbour, 'Fanet Lady'. She's a right ol' bucket but she goes a treat.'

'Who, Mrs. Skidmore?' quipped Mister Duvall, returning the nudge back into Sid's ribs with equal severity.

Although winded, Sid went on to explain that because tomorrow was Sunday it followed that there would be no performance of 'Postcards from the Seaside'. So how would Mister Duvall feel about bringing Emily along for a trip around the bay aboard his boat, hopefully with Gerty being only too happy to make up a social foursome.

Sensing Mister Duvall was dragging his feet Sid had no choice but to add a little sweetener to the bait.

'Listen mate, if you can talk Emily into it you can forget about this week's 'alf a crown,' conceded Sid and needless to say Mister Duvall's quick fire handshake of confirmation nearly removed Sid's arm from its socket.

On the cliff top pathway, en route for his afternoon siesta, Mister Duvall, exhilarated by the purity of the fresh sea air, soon found himself strutting along to the brass band's rousing rendition of the spiritually uplifting *Onward Christian Soldiers*.

Like the schoolboy that at heart he was, as he marched so he sang out loudly and proudly in the firm belief that *Christ the royal master leads against the foe.*

Meanwhile, on the other side of the English Channel, on the beaches of Dunkirk, the British soldiers awaited their fate.

With their backs to the sea they could retreat no further.

CHAPTER 4

BIG ONES SMALL ONES SOME AS BIG AS YER 'EAD!

Back in his room, tucked cosily beneath the sheet and wafer thin blanket, the gentleman of the theatre was trying his utmost to grab a little shut eye before his evening performance but with thoughts of a prospective holiday romance dancing around in his head, Mister Duvall was finding, much to his annoyance, a little difficulty in dozing off. However, being the true thespian that he undoubtedly was, he soon overcame this minor hiccup.

Once awake, out of bed and positioned at the basin, he braced himself for the impending shock. Swishing the cold tap water frantically into his face he then applied whatever lather he could muster from the bone hard remnants of the carbolic soap to carefully layer it upon his chin in readiness for a torturous scrape of the inhouse razor. Venturing the blade up to and under his nostrils, removing any trace of unwanted moustache, Mister Duvall noticed that a dinner plate, covered by an appropriately sized saucepan lid, had been placed upon the table. Wiping away whatever traces of soap remained on his face he lifted the saucepan lid to observe two slices of bread and a not too generous helping of mango chutney staring back at him. However, with the possibility of a lucrative holiday dalliance sending butterflies fluttering around his stomach Mister Duvall returned the saucepan lid back to its protective position.

At the theatre, in the sanctuary of his dressing room, he slung his raincoat over the collapsible table and settled himself down into the wobbly wicker chair. Finding the murmurings of the audience soothing to his ears, it was easy for Mister Duvall to relax but unfortunately, from the backstage area, came Sid's hollering voice to inform all concerned that it was 'Five minutes to showtime!'

Scrambling from the cosiness of the wobbly chair Mister Duvall lifted the candy striped jacket from the nail on the back of the door and once the jacket was donned, ventured out into the backstage area. He found his arrival coinciding with the hopelessly out of tune piano heralding Sid's grand entrance into the limelight.

'Tonight is landladies' night!' Sid proudly proclaimed to the auditorium before delivering a statement that would incite scowls of mock disapproval from certain members of the audience who were, in all honesty, carrying a fair amount of excess timber about their persons.

'Let me tell you about my landlady,' suggested Sid engagingly. 'My landlady is big, an' when I say big I mean big!' he roared, describing the poor woman's physical attributes by spraying out his arms to their fullest extent.

With neither a thought nor care that these disparaging remarks were describing pretty well every woman present that evening, Sid continued with his tale of woe.

'My landlady is that big, from the front it looks like she's trawlin' for mackerel,' he quipped, pausing in the hope of hefty guffaws, which thankfully arrived smack on cue. Crossing his fingers for luck Sid then spat out what he prayed would be a killer of a punch line. 'An' from the back it looks like she's 'ad a crackin' day!' Reducing the landladies to a condition of howling hysterics it would appear that Sid's prayer had been answered.

But, as the laughter faded, from out of the darkness of the auditorium came the sound of a masculine voice as rough as old boots. 'The Road to Mandalay!' the grumpy voice demanded.

'Who said that?' asked a startled Sid, obviously taken by surprise.

The voice repeated its request, only this time in a much ruder and threatening manner. 'You 'eard, *The Road to Mandalay*!' it growled, and Sid, not used to being heckled, broke into a cold nerve wracking sweat.

'The Road to Mandalay?' stammered a confused Sid, his voice quaking with fright. 'You want me to sing it?'

'No I want you to take it!' yelled the heckler, drawing even more howls of laughter from the landladies.

Mopping his dripping brow Sid took a deep breath and simply got on with the job in hand, which was to deliver good old seaside postcard sauciness and, fortunately for him, Sid had a little more of the required sauce up his sleeve.

'The other mornin' my landlady shouted over to the milkman, 'Ave you got 'alf o' Stork on?' and the milkman shouted back 'No madam, it's the way the wind's blowin' me apron!' he blurted, enticing even more howls of laughter from the ladies.

Standing attentively in the wings, on hearing a shuffling of feet behind him, Mister Duvall turned to come face to face with the Topsy Turvys. Whispered hellos were exchanged before the two Pierrot clowned cuties mounted the four wooden steps to await Sid's proclamation

'Ladies and gentlemen,' Sid then exclaimed, ''ere they are, the Topsy Turvys!'

Never slow in coming forward, with enthusiasm in abundance, the Topsy Turvys came bounding into the limelight to present their audience with yet another bucketful of overly rehearsed cornball which would send Mister Duvall returning in his dressing room to add whatever finishing touches were required in regard to his presentation before he was back up the wooden steps just in time to hear the Topsy Turvys launch into their grand announcement.

'A gentleman who has been singing on the wireless with Billy Cotton,' they stated proudly and in perfect unison, 'coming directly from the Brighton 'Ippodrome, where he has been sharing the stage with the one and only Max Miller, ladies and gentlemen we give you Mister Lester Duvall!'

Striding onto and around the hallowed boards for a few seconds, embracing the hearty greeting that the landladies were bestowing upon him, throwing his arms into the air Mister Duvall rather cheekily announced, 'For all you lovely landladies out there, a little ditty entitled *Don't go back down the mines dad, there's plenty of slack in your pants*!'

This was music indeed to the ears of the landladies. Raising his straw boater to lightly drum its brim cheekily on his forehead, the gentleman of the theatre commenced delivery of a highly emotional monologue.

Listen to my story so sad but it is true.
It happened to my grand dad, could so easily have been you.
He was working at the brewery, stirring up the jungle juice
But fell orf the plank into the tank. Well that was his excuse.
The thing about my grand dad was he never learned to swim
He went into the gurgly stuff and that was the end of him.

But the sympathetic sighs that these moving words had generated from the landladies were about to transform into uncontrollable fits of laughter.

He was two hours drowning. Where did he go amiss?
There was doubt 'cause he climbed out five times for a gypsy's kiss! (Gypsy's kiss/ piss)

Again this typical postcard humour proved itself the ideal fodder to tickle the fancies of the landladies and only as their joyous laughter began to fade, did Mister Duvall turn to the old chap seated at the piano. He was heard to request 'Music, maestro please?' and, with the pianist playing the introduction for *Postcards From The Seaside*, Mister Duvall went soft shoe shuffling around the stage, conveying his words to the by now captivated audience.

He sends her postcards from the seaside
Warm greetings and beside crossed kisses he wishes she were there.

As he sang so his eyes scanned around the auditorium in search of Emily but the first familiar face he spotted was that of Gerty Skidmore. Despite the fact that this was the first time he'd seen her head without its flowery turban Mister Duvall recognised her immediately. Unfortunately Gerty's face had the expression *bored stiff* written all over it. Still being the trooper that he was Mister Duvall carried on regardless and it would be on arrival at the concluding line that his heart skipped a beat. Seated maybe four or five rows back, he spotted a mesmerised Emily.

Bowing and scraping to the well-deserved applause, at the appropriate moment, the gentleman of the theatre raised his head to step forward and once again deliver the words of wisdom that had worked so beautifully the previous evening.

'Ladies and gentlemen,' Mister Duvall said, gesturing for calm. 'Let us not forget the awful traumas our brave boys are experiencing as they retreat onto the beaches of Dunkirk, situated just twenty odd miles or so across the English Channel.'

In the full knowledge that he was on solid ground, the gentleman of the theatre continued to lead his audience down the path of emotional blackmail.

'So tonight, before we drift into golden slumbers,' he pleaded, drawing ecclesiastical inspiration by keeping his delivery akin to the style of a Southern State evangelist, 'I urge you all, each and every one of you, to join me in prayer! Indeed let us all pray together that our boys will soon be home, seated around the fireside with their families and loved ones!'

A spiritual hush descended around the auditorium. Half way up the middle gangway, to his right, a middle-aged and somewhat overweight lady managed to rise from her aisle seat. 'Gawd bless you Mister Duvall!' she hollered, resulting in a standing ovation from all but one the landladies, the exception being a certain Gerty Skidmore.

At his stage door posting Sid sat scrawling the evening's box office figures into his little red note book when the sound of tapping on the door disturbed his concentration. Quickly returning the notebook to his pocket Sid rose to be greeted by the stunning sight of Emily. Wearing a light blue box coat that hung loosely over a navy polka dot dress, the young lady was an absolute joy to behold.

'Come on in darlin',' said Sid, 'Mister Duvall won't be long. 'E's just scrapin' the slap orf 'is boat.*(Boat race/face)* Now I don't suppose Mister Duvall 'as mentioned a little sailin' trip tomorrow by any chance?' Sid teasingly inquired, rubbing his grubby hands in anticipation.

'A sailing trip, tomorrow?' asked a bemused Emily. 'No, Mister Duvall hasn't said word but, there again, we only met this morning.'

'Well let me tell you young lady, Mister Duvall is insistin' you accompany 'im on a trip round the bay with me and Gerty Skidmore!' Sid gleefully enthused, blurting out the details of the ensuing adventure aboard 'Thanet Lady' but the brash arrival of Mrs Skidmore drew the sting from out of his enthusiasm.

'So apparently we're all sailin' around on the bubbly waves tomorrow, like the one big 'appy family we supposedly are,' Gerty said with a hint of sarcasm that happened to coincide with the emergence of Mister Duvall from his dressing room.

'And 'ere 'e is,' Gerty mockingly announced. 'A song, a smile, and a surgical truss. Yes it's the geezer himself, Mister Lester Duvall!'

'Oh Lester, you were wonderful tonight! Emily exclaimed, hardly containing her excitement before quickly levelling her praise of the show. 'And as for the Topsy Turvys, weren't they just absolutely hilarious!'

'Me sides is still achin'' tutted Gerty, patting the back of her hair whilst wiggling her shoulder blades.

Ignoring Gerty's jibe, Mister Duvall took it upon himself to make the necessary introductions. 'Mrs Skidmore may I introduce Miss Emily Bagshaw? Miss Bagshaw, Mrs Skidmore,' said the gentleman of the theatre, gesturing to each lady appropriately. Turning to Sid he then asked the question 'I presume that Emily is aware of our little soiree tomorrow afternoon?'

With a nod of the head Sid confirmed that all necessary arrangements were in place, and a wry smile indicated that hope, indeed great expectations, of a highly sensuous nature might well be heading his way.

Emily's nature was to be well mannered at all times and she therefore held out her hand for Gerty to shake. 'I'm very pleased to meet you Mrs Skidmore,' she said courteously.

Rudely turning her face away from the younger lady a brisk 'Likewise I'm sure,' was all that Gerty was prepared to give but, undeterred, Emily continued down the path of polite conversation.

'Lester tells me that you're his landlady,' she said, only for Gerty's response to be equally as short and stabbing as the previous one.

'Yeah, that's right,' Gerty replied, indicating that she couldn't care less.

Sensing that an air of jollity was called for, the gentleman of the theatre was quick to intercept Gerty's stinging attitude.

'Actually Miss Bagshaw is staying with her aunt who lives, would you believe, at Waterloo House, that rather grand place next door to the Spotted Dog,' he announced, endeavouring to talk up Emily's social standing. He should have known better.

'Hit's all right for some!' mocked Gerty in an over the top posh tone that had its emphasis on the 'H'. 'I pull the pints at the Spotted Dog now and again. You'll 'ave to pop round one night,' she snidely suggested. 'Bring your aunt and ol' Burlington Berty 'ere with you. We'll all 'ave a right ol' ding dong *(Ding dong/sing song)*.'

That comment of Gerty's would be, as far as Mister Duvall was concerned, the straw that broke the camel's back. In short he blew his top.

'Mrs Skidmore,' he retorted, 'you have been told, in no uncertain terms, that I do not drink and as far as I'm aware, neither does Miss Bagshaw!'

Gerty flexed her shoulders and prepared for the inevitable. She didn't have too long a wait.

'That is to say Miss Bagshaw and I, have absolutely no intention of ever stepping foot into such a down-trodden hovel as the Spotted Dog!' snapped Mister Duvall, angrily spitting out words that would, for the very first time in her life, silence Gerty.

Taking advantage of the moment to bid Sid goodnight, Mister Duvall informed him that 'Miss Bagshaw and I look forward to seeing you tomorrow, twelve noon on the quayside.'

Politely wishing both Gerty and Sid goodnight, Emily followed Mister Duvall out into the evening air.

After a short period of maybe four of five seconds Mister Duvall's head reappeared back around the stage door to address Gerty.

'Don't wait up, I have my own key!' he sneered before closing the door with a mighty crash.

'Who the 'ell's he fink 'e is!' roared Gerty in apparent disbelief.

'Give the bloke a chance,' urged Sid. ''E's a bit poncified I'll grant yer but 'is kind always are. In my book Mister Lester Duvall is a true gentleman o' the featre.'

'Oh 'e's poncified alright,' she replied. 'Poncified enough to put me in the waitin' room for this week's rent.'

Sid immediately went into shock horror mode. 'But Mister Duvall told me 'e paid you a week up front!' he gasped in amazement. 'That's why 'e's brassic *(Borassic lint/skint)*!'

'Well let me tell you somethin',' Gerty snapped, putting Sid in his place. 'That so called gentleman o' the featre ain't paid me nothin'! Not a bleedin' penny!'

Bringing Gerty close to him, with his facial stubble scraping against the softness of her powdered cheek, Sid opened up his heart.

'I fink a lot o' you Gerty,' he sighed, gently stroking the nape of her neck, his lips journeying north to where his off-white

36

teeth began to sensually nibble at the lobe of her ear. ''Ow's about me an' you 'avin' the last one down the Spotted Dog?'

Sadly this flirtatious suggestion was met by a non responsive Gerty easing herself away from him in double quick time.

'On second thoughts I think I'll give the Spotty a wide berth tonight,' Sid disappointingly sighed, lowering his head in dark despair.

'Come 'ere you randy ol' git,' chuckled Gerty, aiming a smacker of a kiss that landed perfectly onto his bald pate.

Always the gentleman Sid graciously held the stage door open for the lady to pass through and could only look on helplessly as Gerty disappeared into the still of the night. Sadly for him the slightest movement was pure agony as the poor chap was literally crippled with frustration.

CHAPTER 5

HELLO! WHO'S YOUR LADYFRIEND?

In the moonlight, as they strolled towards the bandstand, Emily felt a gentle pat on her arm.

'I must apologise most profusely for Mrs Skidmore's behaviour this evening,' said Mister Duvall in good old upper lip fashion.

'That's very kind of you Lester but there's really nothing to apologise for,' said Emily, seizing the opportunity to bestow more words of praise upon him 'But I will say this to you Mister Lester Duvall, you are one very talented gentleman.'

'Yes I know,' he modestly replied, guiding Emily to a nearby bench just off the pathway, in front of the bandstand, and which he'd noted earlier as being an ideal spot for night time seduction.

'And would Billy Cotton be aware that you are here in Thanet for the summer season?' Emily queried as she took a seat.

'Oh most certainly!' was his emphatic reply. 'Why I was lunching with Mister Cotton only last week and consequently I now find myself being the main topic of conversation in the BBC canteen,' bragged Mister Duvall, seating himself down alongside of her.

Obviously thrilled to be in the presence of such grandeur, Emily squeezed Mister Duvall's arm excitedly but when she mentioned the fact that the chill of the evening was proving a little uncomfortable for her the gentleman of the theatre foolishly interpreted this to be a green light to advance.

Maybe it was the fragrance of her California Poppy perfume that was causing his lustful desires to spiral out of control.

Bringing her closer, he moved in for the kill. His hands were now established inside her box coat and, with his chin resting upon her shoulder the sight of Gerty Skidmore wending her way home did prove a little off putting but insufficiently to cool the hot sensations that were stirring wildly in his nether regions. Bringing Emily even closer, as his eager lips brushed slowly against hers his hands began to familiarise themselves with the layout of the front of her polka dotted dress. His hands roamed freely over the contours of her tiny breasts until a slight hiccup temporarily upset the applecart by way of a couple of wretched tortoise shell buttons. Luckily his supple fingers enjoyed instant success as the first button surrendered itself with comparative ease.

The devil in his soul was now gunning for a full house but Emily's resistance suddenly reared its head to make its presence known in no uncertain terms.

'Do you mind?' she gasped 'We've only just met,' springing to her feet in protest whilst Mister Duvall, via his trouser pocket, frantically readjusted himself.

Briskly, Emily refastened her top button and set about completing the remaining one hundred yards or so to the door of Waterloo House with a humbled Mister Duvall walking somberly beside her. Not one word was to pass between them until Emily eventually broke the silence.

'I would invite you in for cocoa but my aunt just would not approve,' she stated abruptly, obviously still displeased with Mister Duvall's advances.

'Do I look like some murderous Nazi?' queried Mister Duvall, jesting mildly only for Emily to answer with a rather searching question of her own.

'May I ask how old you are?' she inquired in not too friendly a tone.

'As a matter of fact I've just turned thirty,' Mister Duvall answered and waited for the obvious 'well you certainly don't look it' comment to arrive.

With that comment never materialising, Mister Duvall had no option but to prompt her. 'Is my age such a problem?' he warily asked

But Emily was now taking a more serious stance, informing him that her aunt would be of the opinion that he, being a fit and healthy gentleman of a certain age, should be over there.

Mister Duvall shook his head in confusion. 'Over where?' he asked in slight bewilderment.

'Over there, with our boys!' Emily shrieked, pointing in the direction of the English Channel. 'Doing your bit, as brother Bertie did at the Somme!' she snapped, revealing just how ruffled her feathers were and when Mister Duvall offered nothing in the way of defence Emily chose to qualify her annoyance.

'We Bagshaws enjoy a fine military history,' she stated proudly. 'I'll have you know that great grandpapa served alongside Wellington at Waterloo, that being the very reason our family house bears the name Waterloo!' she said, driving her point home most emphatically.

Whether Mister Duvall liked it or not there was more Bagshaw family history heading his way but before he could even think of anything to say Emily, guns blazing, was at him again.

'Grandpapa was at Balaclava with Lord Cardigan! And before you ask, no, he wasn't just sitting there knitting!' she exclaimed in frustration.

Waiting a few seconds for calm to prevail, with his shoulders back the gentleman of the theatre chose the wording of his response most carefully. 'Is your aunt aware that I am Mister

Lester Duvall, of the Brighton Hippodrome no less, and who has enjoyed, and on several occasions I might add, second billing to Max Miller!'

Pausing for composure the gentleman of the theatre then coolly pitched his killer of a closedown line. 'And I'm not even going to mention Billy Cotton.'

Silence again ensued before Emily, feeling a tad guilty and, in an effort to rekindle any sign of the flame that had flickered between them, offered a form of an apology.

'Oh Lester I've hurt and offended you and I really didn't mean to,' she said, hesitating nervously, 'but it's simply that the theatrical profession can hardly be regarded as respectable,'

Mister Duvall's face drained with over the top expressional hurt but Emily, although sympathetic, nevertheless continued with her assassination of his character.

'Your chosen profession, honourable as it may be, really cannot be seen in the same light as that of, say, a doctor or a lawyer. Indeed brother Bertie, who incidentally has, on occasion, found Max Miller to be very funny, would take the view that a career in the theatre would be an unsavoury choice of occupation.'

Reaching out to take her hand Mister Duvall lowered his head. 'But that doesn't alter my feelings for you my darling,' he sighed, making use of the well used sloppy response that had dug him out of many a hole more times than he'd had hot dinners.

'Nor mine for you,' whispered Emily, glancing his cheek with a kiss.

'Then I will call at your door twelve noon on the dot,' suggested Mister Duvall, only to find Emily still in a somewhat apprehensive mood.

'I would prefer we meet at the harbour entrance,' she cautiously replied.

Knowing deep down that what the little lady really meant to say was 'I'd rather my aunt didn't see you,' but not wishing to pursue the matter further, Mister Duvall again took Emily reassuringly in his arms and this time the little lady offered little resistance. Kissing her fully on the lips, the gentleman of the theatre was allowed the divine pleasure of wallowing in the taste of sticky Regimental Red lipstick before Emily released herself from his most sensuous but well behaved embrace.

'The harbour at noon my darling,' he romantically sighed.

Softly squeezing Mister Duvall's hand Emily walked away. At the front door of Waterloo House she turned and blew him a goodnight kiss.

Seemingly forgiven for breaking the unwritten law of trying it on as soon as the first night, wearing his heart upon his sleeve, Mister Duvall celebrated his good fortune by literally dancing across Waterloo Street. Those tortoise shell buttons had an awful lot to answer for.

Carefully inserting his key into the lock of number 65, Mister Duvall was fully aware that absolute silence would be called for. Gently easing the front door open he tiptoed inside to bring the door to a near silent close. In order to avoid any creaking from the stairs he was about to remove his shoes when, from out of the semi darkness of the candlelit kitchen Gerty's acidic tones came filtering through. 'Bit of a kissin' match goin' on out there,' she sneered.

'Mrs Skidmore!' he angrily retorted. 'Were you spying on me?'

But Gerty, cool as a cucumber, invited him to 'Take off yer coat, sit down and 'ave a drink?'

Hanging his raincoat in the hallway Mister Duvall stepped into the kitchen to once again plead sobriety. 'How many more times do you need telling?' he retorted. 'I do not drink and…' but before he could finish this angry rant of his was brought to a halt by a tea towel being hurled into his face.

'Wipe yer bracket on that,' Gerty commanded. 'Look at yer, caked in all 'er fancy lippy.'

Hesitating for a few seconds Mister Duvall dutifully obeyed. Returning the towel to the draining board he sat down at the table whilst Gerty gave his face an unexpected going over. 'Mmm that'll 'ave to do for now,' she muttered.

Picking up the gin bottle Gerty poured a healthy tot into her teacup. Demolishing the measure in one mighty gulp, she wiped her gin-soaked lips with the back of her hand to go eyeball to eyeball with the gentleman of the theatre.

'So 'ow old did you tell 'er ladyship you was?' hiccupped Gerty.

Giving what he thought would be received as an honest answer Mister Duvall arose from his chair. 'None of your business madam, but,' he angrily snapped, 'if you must know I've just turned thirty! And if that will be all, thank you and goodnight!'

But it wasn't to be all. Gerty had an ace up her sleeve that would be produced when the appropriate moment presented itself.

'So what year were you born?' she wickedly asked.

Understandably puzzled Mister Duvall returned himself to the table to utter a flustered reply. 'Well it's 1940 now and, well, yes, let me see, mm, I'm thirty, years that is, and so that would mean,' he drawled, attempting, in infantile fashion, to count down the years by the use of his stubby fingers. 'Let me get this right, I was born in… in…' but Gerty, like a lion sensing a free lunch, verbally pounced upon him.

'You were born in 1905,' she stated, stabbing a finger into his face. 'By my reckonin' that makes you firty five.'

Fidgeting nervously Mister Duvall could only reply that he was feeling 'rather uneasy about all this.'

The appropriate moment had presented itself. 'Uneasy?' Gerty queried, about to play her ace card. 'I bet you're feelin' uneasy, Mister Lester Duvall, gentleman o' the bleedin' featre! What a load o' cobblers! *(Cobblers' awls/balls)* I know you; you're Charlie Scrannage!'

'Good Lord!' he gasped, his mouth opening in shock horror.

'You're Charlie Scrannage!' she bawled, continuing to point an accusing finger at him. 'It's you ain't it, Charlie Scrannage, from Befnal Green!'

With barely a second to respond Mister Duvall submitted a plea of not guilty on all counts. 'Madam I have absolutely no idea as to whom you are referring. This fellow, what did you say his name was, Scrannage? Never heard of him!' he shouted, giving the table a resounding thump to drive home his plea of innocence.

But Gerty, like a dog with a bone, was refusing to let go.

'Shout and bawl all you like mate but I'm right ain' I?' she chuckled, pouring herself another shot of gin. 'You're good ol' Charlie Scrannage from Befnal Green.'

Like Simon Peter two thousand years before, Mister Duvall went into denial three times on the bounce but the intense pressure that was being inflicted upon him was becoming impossible to bear.

'So Reggie worn't your ol' man then?' Gerty sneered in the full knowledge that she had the poor blighter pinned helplessly on the ropes and it was then that Mister Duvall, in sheer panic, foolishly broke the golden rule of verbal combat. He retaliated when he should have kept shtum.

'No! No! My dad was Arthur! Arthur Scrannage!' he bellowed, realising immediately that he was about pay dearly for his mistake.

'Got yer!' exclaimed Gerty, throwing her arms victoriously into the air.

Pausing for a few moments to assess the damage Mister Duvall calmed before replying. 'Arthur was my ol' man. Reggie Scrannage was my uncle, my dad's brother. So now you know the truth,' he sighed, indicating surrender. 'Now Gerty, if you'd pour me a drop of that jungle juice,' he said, nodding at the gin bottle, 'I'd be eternally grateful'

Rewarded with a near full tea cup of mothers ruin Mister Duvall took further advantage of Gerty's hospitality by draining the cup's contents in one fell swoop to then discourteously rattle the emptied cup on the table. With that demand immediately fulfilled he again emptied the cup with one mighty swallow and, leaning back into his chair, closed his eyes to wallow in the divine sensation of the alcohol seeping its way into his blood stream. Once satisfied the gentleman of the theatre then opened is eyes to ask the blindingly obvious. 'Right, let's have it, who's been talking?'

'Nobody, I figured it out meself,' replied Gerty. 'I always thought there was somethin' not quite right about you but what clinched was tonight at the featre. That joke you done about your granddad workin' down the brewery, fallin' in the beer and climbin' out for a gypsy's *(gypsy's kiss/piss)*. I fought it's 'im, it's Charlie Scrannage!'

'But I've been using that old chestnut for years,' mused Mister Duvall, holding out his emptied cup in true Oliver Twist style.

Reaching into the top drawer of the sideboard Gerty produced another half bottle of gin but as she unscrewed the top from the bottle she broke into a fit of the giggles. 'That one about your granddad, it was always your party piece Charley boy.'

'And the good ones never leave us, Gerty,' mused Mister Duvall, indicating for her to perform the honours.

'You and my Billy was the best o' mates at school,' said Gerty, pouring more gin into their cups. 'That's 'ow I know 'ow old you are.'

'Billy Skidmore,' Mister Duvall sighed, shaking his head at the recollection of his long lost pal. 'I haven't seen Billy for years. What's he up to these days?' he asked excitedly.

'Search me, 'e's cleared orf with the barmaid from the Spotted Dog,' Gerty replied with a shrug of her shoulders.'

'Oh yes, of course he has,' was Mister Duvall's light hearted comment before delving deep to frantically search through the dustbins of his memory

'Gerty Skidmore? Gerty Skidmore?' Mister Duvall kept muttering to himself. 'For the life of me I can't recall a Gerty Skidmore,' he finally conceded.

'You wouldn't,' Gerty told him. 'In them days I was Gerty Duggins.'

'Gerty Duggins? Gerty Duggins?' he was asking himself, pondering over the name until suddenly his face lit up like a Christmas tree. 'You're dirty Gerty! Of course, dirty Gerty from number thirty!'

'Well you should know Charlie boy. Ooh the things we got up to in them days!' she laughed and, with Mister Duvall still smiling, Gerty enquired if he'd ever had the urge to revisit Bethnal Green for old time's sake.

'Sadly there can be no going back, not for me anyway,' sighed Mister Duvall regretfully as the smile faded from his face. 'Maisy Gumbley and I got a little too close, if you know what I mean.'

Knowing exactly what he meant Gerty pointed an accusing finger. 'I know Maisy was up the duff and you done a runner.'

His guilty expression was telling Gerty that she'd overstepped the mark but it was own up time for both parties.

'You know I always fancied you more than Billy. That's why I let you get your leg over,' said Gerty with a glint in her eye. 'You do remember don't you Charlie boy?' she asked in high expectation.

Sadly Mister Duvall's raised eyebrows indicated that he had no recollection whatsoever of frolicking in the grass with the then Gerty Duggins, not that there was a blade of grass in Bethnal Green to go a frolicking in.

'Maisy's two brothers went lookin' for you,' Gerty reminded him and Mister Duvall, sipping his gin, nodded to indicate that he'd always been aware of the two thugs hot on his tail.

'So where exactly did you get to Charlie boy?' Gerty quizzed. 'One minute you're 'appy as Larry an' the next you've scarpered *(Scarpa Flow/go)* for it.'

According to the gospel of Duvall, Southend on Sea had been his first port of call, where he sought sanctuary from the vengeful Gumbley brothers.

'Soufend!' exclaimed Gerty 'what the 'ell was a bloke like you doin' in Soufend?'

'Blacking up and doing all the Al Jolson songs,' was his cool reply.

Emptying his cup of its content with the expectancy of a refill about to happen, Mister Duvall continued to unravel the details of his rise to celebrity status. A life changing moment had occurred when a fellow entertainer slipped him the wink that there were far more lucrative opportunities to be had in the pubs along Brighton seafront, the popular south coast holiday resort.

'I made haste for Brighton where I became Mister Lester Duvall,' he explained in the flowery tone that so becomes a true gentleman of the theatre.

'And talkin' all la di da an' posh,' said Gerty. 'Give it a rest Charlie boy.'

'But this is precisely how we theatricals parlez, especially in Brighton,' explained the voice of countless stage appearances and wireless broadcasts.

'And that's 'ow you met up with Max Miller, at the Brighton 'Ippodrome was it?' Gerty asked, only to receive an answer that she wasn't quite expecting.

'You tell me, Gerty,' he shrugged. 'I make it all up as I go along.'

'You mean all this Max Miller business is a load o' cobblers?' Gerty gasped.

Mister Duvall simply nodded to confirm.

'And what's all this about you singin' on the wireless with Billy Cotton?' pleaded Gerty, as if begging him not to kill all further illusion.

'It is simply what my audience wishes to hear,' answered Mister Duvall flippantly, only for Gerty to rattle her knuckles on the table in mock anger.

'And so, Mister la di da gentleman o' the bleedin' featre, 'ave I got a bone to pick with you,' teased Gerty playfully quizzing him. 'What's this about you spendin' all yer 'ard earned on a new striped blazer an' straw boater?' she giggled, shoving her face into his. 'I've seen it with my very own eyes Charlie an' its two bob tat. So out with it, where did yer fieve it from?'

'The Brighton Players Amateur Dramatic Society if you must know,' shrugged Mister Duvall before asking the question of what the hell brought her and Billy Skidmore to the Isle of Thanet in the first place.

'It would've been just after you 'opped it out o' Maisy Gumbley's way,' Gerty began. 'I was sweet seventeen an' never bin kissed an' the next thing I know is me an' Billy was 'itched,' she said, sounding none too pleased about the whole affair. 'Billy reckoned there was a few bob in the cockles and whelks game so we upped sticks and moved down 'ere.'

'So what happened with the cockles and whelks?' enquired Mister Duvall, guessing that something untoward was about to be revealed.

'There was this bloke Billy befriended in the Spotted Dog. Billy tapped 'im for some start up cash but once Billy 'ad the bloke's spondoolicks in his back pocket, well, that was that, no more mention of any cockles an' whelks stall,' tutted Gerty, and with an ashamed lowering of her head she veered away from the subject. 'I can't speak too 'ighly o' Sid. 'E's always pointin' the featre people in my direction.'

'So this so called friend of Billy's, did he ever get his money back?' asked Mister Duvall, bringing the conversation back on course.

'What do you think?' Gerty answered. 'I still see the poor bloke around. 'E's the scruffy ol' geezer what walks 'is donkeys up the prom late afternoonish.'

Gerty paused for a moment. 'Billy Skidmore is a selfish connivin' git. Bit like you really,' she chuckled, nodding at Mister Duvall.

Shuffling uncomfortably in the chair, he did not reply. Picking up the gin bottle, Gerty tightened the screw top and returned the bottle to the sideboard's top drawer.

'Drink up Charlie boy,' she more or less commanded, gesturing towards the stairs and handing him one of the saucers containing a lit candle.

'You'll find my room up the top o' the dancers *(Dancing bears/stairs)*. If I ain't up in two minutes, start without me.'

Horizontal refreshment with one's landlady was always considered to be theatrical tradition that could result in a gentleman being awarded either a badge of honour or one of courage but rising tipsily from the chair Mister Duvall didn't seem at all bothered as to which way the pendulum swung. Contemplating the wobbly ascent to paradise he had completed just half a dozen or so steps when he received an eye watering warning from Gerty.

'Don't get danglin' yer best friend in the guzzunder!' she hollered from the bottom of the stairs. 'I ain't emptied the Dettol out yet!'

On entering Gerty's boudoir, Mister Duvall placed the saucer and candle on her dressing table and kicked off his shoes. Attempting to remove his socks he found himself hopping from one foot onto the other until suddenly he fell backwards to land awkwardly, staked out across the double bed.

Gazing up at the ceiling he broke into an uncontrollable fit of the giggles.

'Forgive me Billy for what I'm about to get up to with your missus,' he chuckled, seeking consolation from his old pal.

Finally succeeding in the removal of his socks and now back on his feet, Mister Duvall juggled with the waist button on his flannels. Allowing them to drop to the floor he stepped out and away from them to act upon Gerty's advice in regard to the Dettol. Applying the utmost due care and attention whilst utilising the chamber pot his joyous relief was marred by the sound of an angry exchange of words ringing up from the street below.

Returning the receptacle back to its rightful place beneath the bed he positioned himself a little away from the window to observe the landlord of the Spotted Dog evicting a drunken customer from his premises. A swift hook to the side of the customer's head by the landlord was followed with a clenched fist that smacked sickeningly into the poor chap's jaw, and worse was to come. Not content with completion of the eviction the landlord honed in on his victim who, by now, was collapsed on the pavement directly outside the front door of Waterloo House. With the vilest of language spewing from his mouth, the brute of a landlord proceeded to give his semi-conscious customer a most unmerciful kicking, more or less guaranteeing the poor fellow a one way ticket to Palookaville.

Suddenly, from the room above the front door of Waterloo House, a bedroom light came on, causing a startled Mister Duvall to spring well back and out of sight. He could only listen as more foul-mouthed profanities, presumably from the drunken man, echoed around Waterloo Street before fading into the distance. Emily had been quite correct. The clientele of the Spotted Dog was the lowest of the low.

Easing himself into the comfort of Gerty's double bed Mister Duvall laid down his weary head on the pillow and, after a short period of meditation, came to terms with the fact that he was there to perform a selfless duty in accordance with the ways of a gentleman. Indeed he would adopt the approach that had served him well over the years in such matters. And if that approach had been good enough for Maisy Gumbley then it would be good enough for every other lady on the planet, Miss Emily Bagshaw being the exception.

Gerty entered the bedroom and placed her candle and saucer upon the dressing table alongside Mister Duvall's, dousing both candles as she did so. His eyes were now fixed upon Gerty as she disrobed, fully aware of what her silhouetted figure was doing to his nervous system. With her ample breasts flopping loosely and without out any trace of inhibition whatsoever, Gerty approached the bed as Mister Duvall realised that his tried and trusted formula of female seduction was about to go flying out of the window.

Snuggling up beside him Gerty, landing a smacker of a kiss squarely upon his lips, was quick to take full advantage of the warmth that Mister Duvall's naked body was radiating by running her ice cold feet up and down his legs. Engulfing him with her equally cold hands a brief session of teasing his nipples was abandoned as her exploratory fingers rapidly plunged into descent, coming to rest in that sacred place where angels, if they have any sense, fear to tread.

'Peter's a bit soft tonight Charlie boy,' she whispered, fumbling with his manhood.

Being a man of virility he saw no real cause for concern and without too much further ado the gentleman of the theatre became ready, willing and, as Gerty was about to discover, extremely able.

Mister Lester Duvall may well have been a rogue but in the privacy of Gerty's boudoir he was a tradesman. As her fingernails sunk sensually into the skin on his shoulder blades so Mister Duvall, whispering 'Gently Bentley' to himself, proceeded to demonstrate skills that would compare favourably to those of a precision grinder, causing Gerty to shriek wildly with the pleasure of it all. Nibbling merrily away on her hardened nipples, as his rhythmic strokes kicked into overdrive, so Mister Duvall adhered to the golden rule of *ladies first*, making sure that the customer would always be satisfied.

For a fair few breathless moments they lay motionless, with a spent Mister Duvall casting the odd glance out of the window and over to Waterloo House, to the room above its front door where he presumed Emily lay sleeping.

That was until Gerty's voice broke the silence.

'What you doin' round these parts Charley boy?' she asked.

'If you must know I had to vacate Brighton pretty quickly,' he replied. 'But out of darkness comes the light. By chance I heard about this little number with the Topsy Turvys so, I jumped on the rattler and here I am!'

'So is it's nothin' to do with the Gumbley brothers then?' she suspiciously asked.

'No, but everything to do with the Brighton Players Amateur Dramatic Society wanting their clobber back,' he chuckled.

Returning her head to the warmth of his chest Gerty closed her eyes and drifted into sleep, leaving Mister Duvall alone with his thoughts. In the still of the night feelings of guilt encumbered his mind. This situation he now found himself in was wrong, so very wrong but it would be the rumbling of his stomach that alerted him to the fact that in his room, one floor below, a plate of bread and pickles awaited consumption.

'The story of my life,' he sighed despairingly. 'So near yet so far away.'

CHAPTER 6

DAPPER FROM YOUR NAPPER TO YOUR FEET

With a head that felt like it was about to bid farewell to the rest of his torso, through sleepy eyes Mister Duvall observed Gerty removing various items of clothing from the wardrobe, holding them up for inspection before hanging them upon the picture rail that skirted the room.

'What time is it?' he yawned, stretching out his arms.

'It's 'alf past nine so 'ands orf cocks and on with socks!' hollered Gerty in true sergeant major style before zooming in with a sloppy kiss that landed smack onto his arid lips.

'Up yer get Charlie boy. I've sorted out some o' Billy's clobber for yer,' she said, pointing up to the picture rail as she headed out of the bedroom.

Following a fair degree of huffing and puffing Mister Duvall eased himself from the cosiness of the bed to behold a pair of white canvass tennis pumps laid out for his attention. A light green sleeveless woollen pullover over a white shirt hung from the picture rail next to a pair of brown chequered Oxford Bags that came complete with turn ups. Alongside the baggy trousers hung a double breasted brown jacket, slightly lighter in colour than the Bags and which had, in a previous life, obviously been the other half of a Sunday best suit.

Contemplating a return to bed, Mister Duvall's plan was then halted in its track by Gerty who, armed with a shaving mug, brush and recently boiled kettle, re-entered the bedroom.

Standing before her, naked as the day that he was born, the gentleman of the theatre was quite understandably embarrassed.

'Don't worry Charlie boy, I've seen it all before' Gerty chuckled, pouring most of the hot water into a wash basin upon a small table wedged between the wardrobe and the bucket style whicker chair that was currently playing host to his flannelled trousers.

'We can't 'ave yer smellin' like a pig farm can we now, what with you singin' on the wireless with Billy Cotton,' Gerty sarcastically said, pouring the rest of the hot water into the shaving mug she'd placed upon a beer mat on the corner of her dressing table. Nodding down at Mister Duvall's nether regions Gerty, in the interests of hygiene then proffered a hygienic suggestion. 'Don't forget to whiz the flannel round yer meat an' two veg.'

'This I presume would be Billy's?' asked Mister Duvall, holding up the shaving brush to stroke what remained of the limp bristles.

'Billy won't mind,' stated Gerty, vacating the bedroom.

'Chance would be a fine thing,' he muttered to himself as, utilising the dressing table mirror, Mister Duvall enjoyed the first decent shave he'd had in days.

Having pulled on his underpants he rejoiced in the fact that his socks slid onto his feet a lot easier than they came off and although it carried a rather musty whiff, the white shirt would more than suffice. Granted the cuffs overshot his wrists by a good inch or so but the rolling back of its sleeves would prove the perfect solution and so with the shirt's front buttons fastened Mister Duvall turned his attention to the Oxford Bags. His first avowed intent involved the running of his fingers around the insides of both turn ups but sadly both were bare of coin. With regard to the size of waist and leg measurements, it became apparent that suspension from the shoulders would be necessary. Fortunately, with a blessing from above, he found adjustable bracers to be already buttoned and in place. Shuffling his legs down into the Bags Mister Duvall tucked the shirt deep inside and following a quick dress to the left managed to fasten the fly buttons. Coaxing the bracers into a hovering position above his shoulders he then allowed the bracers to drop, resulting in a stinging whack followed immediately by a facial wince.

Adjusting the bracers upwards, he discovered there was enough play available to bring the crotch of the Bags up to within a whisker of slight discomfort but would ensure the trousers rested perfectly on the top of the tennis pumps. However this adjustment caused much of the shirt to ride up and spill out over his chest granting Mister Duvall the Latino look of a gay caballero but this minor hiccup was overcome by the sleeveless pullover and, with the addition of the double breasted jacket. Mister Lester Duvall thus acquired the necessary image of a true thespian.

'What do you think then Gerty?' he eagerly asked on entry into the kitchen as he launched himself into his 360 degree swivel routine.

'You'll do,' said Gerty, not even bothering to lift her head, 'Sit yerself down'

Picking up a tea towel from the draining board she proceeded to wrap the towel firmly around his neck in true bib and tucker style. Within seconds a plate bearing two fried eggs, two or three rashers of bacon and a slice of fried bread landed in front of him.

'You earned this last night Charlie boy,' she sighed as any well satisfied lady would before lifting the cosy from the pot to pour him a cup of freshly made tea.

'Ah yes, *Charlie boy*. It's all rather awkward isn't it?' sighed Mister Duvall, nibbling rabbit fashion on a slice of fried bread before taking a sip of the hot steaming tea.

Returning the cosy to the top of the teapot, a rather confused Gerty asked, 'Awkward for who, Charlie, you or me?'

'I'm sorry Gerty but you'll to have to ease off the Charlie boy bit,' replied Mister Duvall, shaking his head disapprovingly.

'So what am I 'sposed to call yer? 'I can't keep callin' you Mister Duvall can I?' Gerty giggled. 'Not after what we got up to last night.'

But the gentleman of the theatre was adamant. 'Look Emily's only here until Tuesday, and then she's going home. And that will give me time to think.'

'Think about what? 'Like is it me or 'er?' Gerty asked, sounding not at all pleased.

Gulping a mouthful of the hot tea that very near took the skin from his mouth, Mister Duvall somehow managed to gesture that a calming presence was called for but Gerty was insistent.

'I wanna know exactly where I stand Charlie boy?' she demanded, rapping the table with her knuckles.

The moment of truth had arrived. The gentleman of the theatre had no option but to lay his cards upon the table.

'As you know Miss Bagshaw happens to come from good well-oiled stock,' he stated, immediately wishing the ground would swallow him up.

'You mean she's worth a few bob. Nothin' changes with you, Charlie Scrannage! Always out fer yourself and stuff anybody what gets in yer way!' she snapped, throwing her arms into the air.

Staring down into what remained of his breakfast Mister Duvall refused to be goaded. 'And I hate to remind you Gerty,' he said coolly, 'but you're still Billy Skidmore's wife.'

'Billy's gone and 'e ain't comin' back!' Gerty raved, slamming the table with her fist. 'An' I don't want 'im back neither!'

Sitting motionless Mister Duvall said nothing but as Gerty's hand slowly moved across the table to pick up the bread knife, fearful of what could be the worst possible scenario, he braced himself for confrontation.

Instead Gerty, tucking the loaf under her arm, hacked off a healthy sized doorstep from off the end of the loaf to crash land square onto his plate. Never one to look a gifted horse in the mouth, Mister Duvall then commenced mop up what remained of his breakfast.

'So 'ow's this sound?' Gerty humbly asked. 'Suppose you was to make your bed 'ere?' she suggested, as taking a seat at the table her hand came to rest upon his thigh. 'We could always come to some arrangement about the rent.'

Mister Duvall smiled but did not take the bait, choosing instead to remove the tea towel from around his neck. Dabbing his lips with it he then casually tossed the towel across to where it rightly belonged, on the draining board.

'Let's just enjoy the day,' he stated in exasperation.

Gerty stood up from the table. Feeling that her nose had been pushed firmly out of place she walked into the hallway. Slipping into her boxy brown jacket and armed with her flowery headscarf Gerty emerged back into the kitchen. Not bothering to look at Mister Duvall she pulled open the middle drawer of the sideboard to grasp her handbag when she suddenly becoming aware that Mister Duvall had crept up and was standing behind her.

Removing the handbag and scarf from her hold he placed the items down onto the sideboard and, placing his arms around Gerty's waist, his mouth sought the nape of her neck.

'Don't start me orf again Charlie,' she sighed. 'I'm already late for Sid as it is,' but with his fingers trying their very best to unbutton her white blouse, the sensations were proving a little too hard for Gerty to resist. 'No, please, Charlie, no,' she sighed in ecstasy, which roughly translated meant *yes*.

Whether it was a misinterpretation on his part or not, Mister Duvall immediately released her from his hold. 'Better not be late for Sid then,' he coldly stated.

Picking up her headscarf from the sideboard, Gerty wrapped it over her clipped down hair and knotted the ends tightly under her chin. Checking herself quickly in the sideboard's mirror Gerty sneaked a kiss onto Mister Duvall's cheek before taking hold of the biscuit tin.

'Just some cakes I've baked for us,' she giggled, rattling the tin as she headed out of the house.

Noticing immediately that Gerty had left her handbag on the sideboard in an instant Mister Duvall succumbed to temptation. Snatching at the handbag he unzipped the fastener in double quick time to discover that he'd struck gold. With Gerty's purse staring him in the face there was not a moment to lose. Acting on his feet, he took the decision to loot and scoot. The sky was his limit, the world his lobster and Christmas would be a little early this year, or so he believed.

The sound of a key being inserted into the lock of the front door brought any such criminal intent to a halt. In sheer panic he returned the purse to the handbag and, with the speed of a bullet from a gun, zipped the fastener shut. A moment later

Gerty came bursting into the kitchen to be greeted by the sight of a smiling Mister Duvall waving the handbag at her.

'I was just about to come running after you,' he chuckled convincingly.

'Oh Charlie boy, I'd forget me 'ead if it worn't nailed on!' laughed Gerty, stretching out her arms to him in an exhibition of undeniable gratitude. ''Ow's a nice bit o' beef sound for yer Sunday dinner next weekend?' she suggested temptingly

'It sounds good to me Gerty,' Mister Duvall replied. 'Now, for the last time, let's have no more Charlie boy!'

'I'm sorry, Charlie,' Gerty chuckled, exiting into the hallway, from where she called. 'Oops! Sorry, Charlie! I mean Mister Duvall!' only to pop her head around the kitchen door to make a rather profound statement. 'And if Sid thinks 'e's gettin' his leg over tonight then 'e can think again!'

She laughed before disappearing again, slamming the front door behind her.

Mister Duvall was not laughing. Another five minutes and he would have been out the door and halfway to Margate.

Ascending the stairs at the rate of two at a time, Mister Duvall thundered into Gerty's bedroom to bring down the brown double breasted jacket from its perch on the picture rail, slip his arms into its sleeves, wriggling his shoulders to achieve a near perfect fit. Lifting the shirt's ample collar up and out over the jacket's collar he laid it flat in true summery open-neck style, having decided that the double breasted jacket would be worn unbuttoned.

Returning downstairs to the kitchen the gentleman of the theatre, admiring himself in the sideboard mirror, came to the conclusion that, for a thirty five year old bounder, he wasn't wearing too badly at all. True there were early signs of thinning around the crown but that aside, he remained in possession of a fairly decent thatch.

A bounder, however, is never satisfied.

Seeing off his tea in one final gulp he turned his attention to the sideboard where, with one sharp jerk of its handles, he prised open the top drawer. Ignoring the remnants of the half bottle of gin left over from the night before he proceeded to rummage through an array of cotton wool, odd buttons, hair grips and drawing pins until his hands fell upon a couple of combs, one of them a gentleman's comb. Being fully aware that his healthy mane was about to be pitted against a truly wild sea breeze, the decision was taken with regard to the matter of keeping his hair stuck down firmly to his scalp. Taking the gents' comb from the drawer Mister Duvall, picking up the frying pan from the stove, began dragging the teeth of the comb back and forth slowly through the still warm grease that lay in the base of the pan to be provided with a plentiful scoop of what was, in essence, the poor man's Brylcream. Stooping to bring his face in line with the mirror, legs bent at the knees, the gentleman of the theatre then commenced the delicate process of working the melted lard into his black hair until he was satisfied that, regardless of the raging winds of the Channel, his hair was going nowhere.

Now, with the desired look of a Hollywood heartthrob attained, popping the comb into the jacket's breast pocket he again checked himself in the sideboard's mirror and Mister Lester Duvall, gentleman of the theatre, liked what he saw.

Indeed you could say that everything was spivvingly tickety boo.

CHAPTER 7

EVERYTHING'S BRIGHT AND BREEZY!
DO AS YOU DARN WELL PLEASY!

As if with wings on his heels Mister Lester Duvall, gentleman of the theatre, cleared the four steps in one mighty leap to touch down onto the pavement of Waterloo Street and having made it to the cliff top pathway, with the Oxford Bags flapping around in the breeze, he paused to enjoy the view of the English Channel shimmering beneath a cloudless sky. Yes indeed, his future was looking good.

Dipping rather steeply to wend its way down to the promenade the path would eventually bring Mister Duvall face to face with the harbour entrance. Emily was nowhere to be seen but, his arrival being quite early, there was no cause for concern.

Settling himself shoulder to shoulder with the scoffing customers of the cockles and whelks man he awaited Emily. With the heat of the noon day sun proving uncomfortable, he removed the double breasted brown jacket and then found his attention drawn to just inside the harbour entrance, to where the brass band had, at that very moment, commenced to play the old time music hall favourite *Ship Ahoy*.

One person in particular, a 'down for the day' elderly gent, trousers rolled up to the knees and a knotted at the corners hanky plonked upon his head, had taken the striking up of the brass band as his cue to dance, knees up style, around the band's conductor, a man who was making no secret of his displeasure at being upstaged. Adding further annoyance to the egotistical baton waver, but much to the delight to the gathering crowd, the dancing gent was now enhancing the band's rhythm section by the rattling of a couple of cow bones up and down his cocking legs.

Mister Duvall smiled at the choice of song. *Ship Ahoy* had held pride of place in his very own repertoire when, as a teenaged boy, he himself had performed the song, albeit with a somewhat crude slant on the original lyric, in and around the backstreet pubs of Bethnal Green where East End folk viewed his lewd interpretation as sheer poetry.

In order to obtain a better view of the old chap's impromptu dance session Mister Duvall rose from his seated position but as he did so felt a gentle tap upon his shoulder. There, carrying a picnic basket, its contents neatly covered by a red and white chequered tea cloth, stood Emily. Wearing a cream cardigan over a flimsy white blouse and with a pair of navy blue bell bottomed sailors' pants she was simply radiating casual elegance. In short she looked stunningly beautiful.

To any hot blooded man of a hetero persuasion this breathtaking sight of feminine beauty was more than enough to ignite any flame of lustful desire. Greeting her with a hug just a simple whiff of her California Poppy perfume was enough for Mister Duvall to once again find himself in a 'red rag to a bull' situation but luckily, delving his hand into his trouser pocket, a quick flick of the fingers helped quell the embarrassment.

'Allow me my dear,' said a red-faced Mister Duvall, taking responsibility for the picnic basket as, linking arms the two prospective lovebirds began to march playfully over the quayside cobbles in search of the good ship 'Thanet Lady'. With the basket bobbing merrily around Mister Duvall's lower middle, keeping perfect time with the oom-pah beat of the brass band, it would prove ideal cover for his most personal of predicaments.

The harbour, on that sun drenched Sunday in late May of 1940, literally brimmed with an array of small colourful fishing boats and pleasure cruisers and it was Emily who spotted Sid standing proudly on the deck of a small cabin cruiser. However, as she and Mister Duvall drew closer, it became blindingly apparent that Sid's dear lady of the seas was, to put it mildly, in dire need of tender loving care.

Sid, himself, sported a navy blue blazer with a white shirt accompanied by an almost perfectly tied Paisley polka dot cravat, along with a pair of Sunday best cricket strides matched with off white plimsolls. The Sailor Sam look was completed by a dark blue mariner's cap seated firmly upon his head.

Gerty, free of her boxy jacket but not of the flowery headscarf, her bared arms protruding from the flimsy white blouse, was perched upon a secured wooden bench skirting the stern of the good ship Thanet Lady. Determined to tan her complexion, Gerty, her eyes shut tightly, was aiming her face purposely into the sun.

'So what time is laughin' boy expected?' she lazily sighed when at that very moment a cry of 'Ahoy there Thanet Lady!' bellowed up from the quayside.

'Oh I spoke too soon,' sighed Gerty despairingly, opening her eyes to see Mister Duvall stood at the bottom of the four-foot long gangplank.

''Alt! Who goes there?' shouted Sid, pointing menacingly at the gentleman.

'We are but two stowaways in search of adventure!' Mister Duvall answered with some assurance.

'And you are not German spies actin' on be'alf of 'Err Hadoph 'Itler?' Sid dutifully asked.

'Ve are most certainly not Zsherman spies! Ve are loyal subjects of ze King!' proclaimed Mister Duvall in a cod Prussian accent that concluded with a Nazi heel clicking routine.

Bowing graciously to Emily, Sid proffered a helping hand as she ventured the couple of steps up the treacherous gangplank as Mister Duvall, loaded with the picnic basket, brought up the rear.

Considering the restrictions of his wonky leg Sid hopped down onto the quayside with relative ease to free his craft from the shackles of the quayside capstan and, once back on deck, he hoisted the tiny gangplank hoping for compliments.

Sadly the image Sid had portrayed of Thanet Lady being 'a right ol' bucket' was a little too accurate. In fact the vessel's seaworthiness was questionable indeed but good manners amongst his passengers prevailed.

'I think she's a lovely lady,' Emily stated warmly.

'I'll second that!' hollered Mister Duvall, hardly in a position to disagree as Emily, relieving him of the picnic basket, made the sort of almighty yet innocent faux pas likely to trigger the wrath of Gerty's acidic tongue.

'I hope you don't mind me saying this,' said Emily to Sid, 'but on the side of your boat says Thanet.'

'It says Fanet 'cause that's what it is! T! H! A! N! E! T! Fanet!' roared Gerty, angrily spelling out the cruiser's name.

'Mrs Skidmore!' protested Mister Duvall. 'I will not stand by and allow Miss Bagshaw to be spoken to in that manner!' and rather than fight fire with fire Gerty surprisingly offered what could be seen to be an apologetic climb down.

'Park your arse down 'ere darlin',' she said, patting the vacant space on the wooden bench alongside her and Emily, being the lady that she was, graciously accepted Gerty's offer, leaving Sid to pull back the chequered tea towel that would reveal two biscuit tins. In the first were a few raspberry jam sandwiches whilst the second tin contained a dozen or so fruity biscuits with a bottle filled with lemonade wedged tightly down the side of the basket.

'I made the jam and baked the biscuits myself,' Emily giggled. 'You can thank my aunt for the lemonade.'

'Tell 'em about my cakes Sid,' muttered Gerty, giving him a gentle nudge and with the prospect of a little bit of *the old how's your father* definitely on the cards Sid was only too happy to oblige.

Placing Gerty's cakes alongside Emily's goodies on the dash above the boat's instrument panel, from a side cupboard Sid produced four tin mugs. Quickly concluding that they had never in their entire lives experienced a washing up bowl Emily, in her mind, had already decided to decline whatever was on offer as Sid, two tin mugs in each hand, swirled them round a couple of times before hurling the remains of cold tea leaves overboard.

Distributing a mug apiece to his guests, Sid, again from out of the side cupboard, came up with a bottle of navy rum, prompting Gerty to thrust her tin mug eagerly in his direction and the ancient mariner did not disappoint.

Turning to Mister Duvall, closing an eye and raising an eye brow, in a true Long John Silver burr asked. 'Would you be takin' grog with an' ol' shipmate?'

'No thank you,' replied Mister Duvall. 'I'll be happy with lemonade.'

'As will I,' Emily answered only for Sid to pour a good measure into her mug anyway but not before Gerty, gulping down her shot of rum, smacked her lips and rudely jab her tin mug into Sid's paunch.

'I'll 'ave 'er whack!' she insisted.

Having replenished Gerty's mug Sid raised his own mug high into the air. Adopting the tone of a fairground boxing booth barker, he requested that everyone join with him in a toast.

'Ladeez and gentlemen,' he announced, 'I give you... Blimey,' he gasped, pointing at Mister Duvall's jacket, 'Billy Skidmore's got a coat exactly the same as the one you're wearin'!'

Mister Duvall, the master of conversation diversion, acting at lightning speed, immediately pounced by picking up where Sid had left off. Raising his mug the gentleman of the theatre proudly stated to one and all, 'The toast is Thanet Lady!'

'I'll drink to that!' responded Gerty guzzling at her rum.

'Here here!' Emily cried playfully, bringing the mug almost but not quite to her lips.

'Hoist in the gangplank!' ordered Sid, taking up position at the wheel, completely forgetting that he had already carried out that specific duty five minutes earlier.

Giving the starting knob a few vigorous twists and turns, all of which were accompanied by more than just a smattering of barrack room profanities, Sid's sturdy efforts were eventually rewarded by the nerve grating sound of metal upon metal. Not too loud a bang was then followed by a puff of thick black smoke emitting from the good Lady's rear until slowly but surely the small cabin cruiser heaved and hiccuped before settling into a more gentle momentum as Thanet Lady slipped her moorings.

'To where are we bound skipper?' asked Mister Duvall.

'We'll be sailin' due…well up towards Margate,' replied Sid, his attention now focused one hundred per cent on clearing the confines of the harbour and with Mister Duvall and Gerty marvelling at Sid's nautical expertise, Emily seized upon the opportunity to discreetly tip the contents of her tin mug over the side.

Out on the briny, and with the sun big and shiny, they sailed, Sid steadfast and strong at the wheel whilst Gerty, relaxing on the bench, again aimed her face directly into the strong rays of the afternoon sun.

With shoulders back and his arm firmly around Emily's waist Mister Duvall, noting that Gerty's eyes were well and truly shut, worked his hand gently but naughtily under Emily's cream cardigan to where his fingers began playfully tickling her tummy. Emily, acting blissfully unaware, smiled, allowing her blonde hair to blow wild and free and casting fate to the wind, in this case the sea breeze, Mister Duvall remained upright and proud. Every single hair on his head remained in place.

Straight ahead lay the beaches of Dunkirk and if Thanet Lady had continued on this course for another twenty fives miles or so, the four folks on deck would have witnessed first hand the sight of thousands of British troops as they gathered helplessly upon the beaches to await impending slaughter.

However, having journeyed maybe two hundred yards out from the harbour, Sid turned the wheel of Thanet Lady most positively to his left and set a course that, if he wasn't careful, would put them at the mercy of the Goodwin Sands. Thankfully, after a hundred yards or so, he chose to cut the engine and cool its wings.

'I could murder a tot,' he sighed, reaching down for the bottle of rum and Gerty, refusing to be short changed, thrust her empty tin mug at him.

Taking the weight off his Oxford Bags Mister Duvall seated himself on the bench alongside Gerty, a move that resulted in Sid having to lean awkwardly over the gentleman of the theatre in order to pour, with some accuracy, the grog into Gerty's mug.

However, resting his hand upon Mister Duvall's shoulder for support, Sid suddenly became aware of a somewhat anti-social smell. 'There's a bit of a pen an' ink *(Pen and ink/stink)* round 'ere!' he declared, interspersing his statement with a fair few sniffs.

Far more concerned with her allocation of rum, Gerty chose to ignore whatever was going on around her even though Sid, undeterred, expanded upon his theory. 'I reckon somebody's 'ad a fryin' pan on the go,' he stated, fanning the air with the palm of his hand.

Mister Duvall, as did Emily remained silent. Always a lady, her nostrils never once flinched.

Disappearing below, Sid was to re-emerge with a large cardboard box that, when upturned, would act as a makeshift table whilst Emily, playing mother, spread out the chequered cloth over the upturned box on which the sandwiches, biscuits and cakes would be placed.

'Did I 'ear you say you was goin' 'ome on Tuesday?' spluttered Sid to Emily as he woofed down one of Gerty's cakes.

'Yes I'm afraid so,' sighed Emily, brushing the snowstorm of crumbs from the front of her blouse, 'but I won't forget this day for a long time to come.'

'I think we all will for one reason or another,' replied Sid, smothering his mouth with the tail end of his cravat.

And so the four, munching heartily as they wallowed in the view of the bustling funfair, the donkeys on the beach and the sun worshippers as they either reclined in their deckchairs or ventured a paddle in the sea, not to mention, high above on the cliff top, the theatre.

Bringing himself to attention yet again Sid raised his glass. 'Everybody, please be…'

'Oh for Christ's sake,' interrupted Gerty, clumsily staggering to her feet leaving Sid, with his legs buckling beneath him, to abandon any thought of his proposal.

Coming to rest on the deck's rail the old man of the sea was quick to deliver a diagnosis. 'Blimey this rum packs a wallop,' was his considered opinion.

In normal circumstances this alcohol fuelled condition would have induced hysterical laughter from Gerty, but instead, bringing her index finger to her lips Gerty indicated a request for immediate silence.

'Listen,' she whispered. 'Can you 'ear what the band is playin'?'

All chit chat ceased to the level of silence as, emanating from the promenade, the stirring sound of the brass band came floating their way with every note seeming to ride gently on the sea breeze.

'It's Postcards from the Seaside!' gasped Sid in amazement. 'They're playin' Postcards from the Seaside! Mister Duvall sir, they're playin' your song!'

Begging for a favour from his guest Sid urged 'Give us a rendition while you're 'ere mate.'

'Oh I wouldn't imagine for one moment they're playing in my key,' Mister Duvall rather snobbily replied, but if he thought this wafer-thin excuse would get past Gerty then he would have to think again.

''Ark at ol' big 'ead! They harr not playing in my key!' she sneered, taking a swipe at his phoney middle class pretence. 'For Gawd's sake Charlie boy, just sing the bleedin' song for 'er Ladyship!' you know 'ow she likes it!' she snapped, following up on her statement with one almighty belch.

Mister Duvall, ignoring Gerty's manners, wrapped his arms firmly around Emily's tiny waist. Embracing her as he listened intently to the band, with the ease of a Broadway leading man, Mister Lester Duvall then commenced to sing and, being the showman that he clearly was, so the gentleman of the theatre played to the gallery, and which, in this case, was the clear blue cloudless sky.

'All those kisses he'd be stealing would send her heart a reeling
as the brass band played oompah on the pier.'

Try as he may, Sid could not hold back. Dropping down onto his wonky knee he sprayed out his arms in true Jolson style as Mister Duvall began to resolve his song quite convincingly.

'Postcards from the seaside, warm greetings and beside,'

Gerty, refusing to be excluded from the party, staggered to her feet to not only join in with the song but, with every morsel of breath in her body, she held on to the very last note for far too long and excruciatingly flat as a pancake.

'Postcards from the seaside, wish you were here!'

Though painful to the ear, Gerty's efforts were taken in good spirit, especially by Emily, who had somehow managed to conceal any expression of discomfort. But, alas and alack, the little lady's applause, rapturous as it was, came across as that of a performing seal begging for a fish.

Taking his position back at the wheel Sid demonstrated his intent by spitting into his hands. Rubbing them together quite vigorously he then launched into the procedure of firing

Thanet Lady's motor. As per normal, Sid's initial attempts, accompanied by a barrage of cursing, were doomed to failure until the motor's screeching sound eventually converted into the rhythmical ticking of a Swiss watch.

Smiling warmly at Emily Sid begged forgiveness. ''Scuse my French darlin',' he joked with a wink of his nautical eye.

Sailing his vessel fifty yards or so due east, Sid suddenly turned Thanet Lady's wheel a full ninety degrees to starboard, causing the sea to whoosh wildly behind his three passengers, who, all seated at the stern, were provided not only with all the fun of the fair but a good soaking of the salty stuff for good measure.

With eyes locked into straight ahead mode and hands seemingly welded to the wheel, just as Drake, Raleigh and Nelson had done in days gone by, Sid approached the harbour with trepidation. His heart of oak beating fast and furious Sid was heard to mutter those immortal words 'Steady boy, steady.'

'Will you be okay Sid?' asked a concerned Mister Duvall.

'Listen mate,' slurred Sid. 'When I tell you that I know my way round this 'arbour like the back o' me…'

Bumph! At that very moment the sound of a booming thud resounded around the quayside as the good ship Thanet Lady smacked head on into her berth.

'Who put that wall there?' a shocked Sid demanded to know.

Gerty, having been thrown from her seat, was fortunate to have Mister Duvall close at hand to cushion the impact and not being one to look a gifted horse in the mouth, Gerty lingered to nestle her cheek upon his shoulder.

Having sensed prior to the collision that all on deck was not ship shape and Bristol fashion, Emily had fortunately gripped the bench tightly in anticipation.

And so it fell upon Sid to restore order upon deck. However, reaching out to relieve Mister Duvall of Gerty's body weight he suddenly broke into yet another bout of sniffing.

'Blimey,' he exclaimed, 'there's that stink again! It's a bit reels *(Reels of cotton / rotten)*!'

Mister Duvall did not react and said precisely nothing. Instead he dusted Gerty's face powder from off the front of his sleeveless pullover to bring Emily close, encouraging her to wrap her arms tenderly around his waist. Resting her head on the very spot that Gerty's face had occupied moments prior, Emily gazed lovingly up into Mister Duvall's eyes. Slowly, and with more than a hint of tenderness, her lips roamed sensuously across his cheek in search of his willing lips. Aware that embers of lust were smouldering deep inside the Oxford Bags, Mister Duvall closed his eyes and allowed his fantasy to dance to the sensuous rhythm of Emily's erotic breathing. Now at the point of no return, he was more than happy to surrender as the little lady whispered so sensuously into his ear, 'Lester, will you please get me off this boat before it sinks.'

Nodded to indicate that he understood Mister Duvall adjusted his stance accordingly. Emily picked up his jacket from the bench and held it open for him to slip into and once his hands had wriggled their way inside the jacket's sleeves so the gentleman of the theatre tunnelled them down past the elbows to where his hands finally emerged into daylight.

But it would be the sight of the jacket that was again to fire Sid's memory as he cried out in astonishment. 'Sure as I'm ridin' this white 'orse Gerty, that coat is the other 'alf o' your Billy's whistle *(Whistle and flute/suit)*!'

Gathering up the picnic basket, a red-faced Mister Duvall hurriedly stepped down onto the quayside to assist Emily and once those dainty little feet of hers were safely returned to dry land she smiled up at Thanet Lady. 'Thank you for a lovely day,' Emily sighed.

Mister Duvall went one better. Gently patting the side of the battered old cabin cruiser as if it was the winning horse at the Epsom Derby, he let his feelings be known. 'Farewell madam. I very much doubt if our paths will cross again.'

How could he have been so foolishly wrong?

Still entrusted with the picnic basket Mister Duvall linked arms with Emily to stroll along the quayside, safe in the knowledge that there were to be no more embarrassing moments, only for Gerty to put a spanner into the works.

'Don't you get worryin' Charlie boy,' she called after him, 'I ain't lettin' no cats out o' no bags!'

The gentleman of the theatre kept walking.

At the promenade the two hopeless romantics seated themselves down on the harbour wall with the sole intention of whiling away what remained of the afternoon in the company of the brass band. However as Emily head came to rest upon Mister Duvall's shoulder, she commenced to hum merrily along to the band's rendition of *I do like to be beside the seaside*, so the conductor, a deeply unhappy man at the best of times, with an angry swish of his baton, brought the concert to an abrupt end, and it was easy to see why.

All the 'down for the day' trippers had seemingly vanished into thin air and faced with an audience that consisted of only Mister Duvall, Emily and the cockles and whelks man, who himself was in danger of being arrested for talking to himself, an on the spot decision had been taken to abort the concert.

Apart from the squawking of the overhead gulls the only sound to now be heard was that of tiny bells jingle jangling on the bridles of the four weary homeward-bound donkeys again being ushered along by the battered trilby wearing, cane swishing smelly little old chap. What had earlier been a noisy and bustling promenade was now a haven of peace and tranquillity, until Sid and Gerty made their presence known.

'Bright 'n' breezy, goes up easy!' Sid cackled raucously as he and Gerty emerged from the harbour quayside. Tears of uncontrollable laughter went cascading down his face as Gerty, hoisting her skirt way past her knickers, attempted an enthusiastic but extremely clumsy interpretation of the Parisian Can Can.

What Sid was singing was the rude, lewd and extremely crude version of the old time music hall song *Ship Ahoy*, the very same parody that had fired Mister Duvall's recollections earlier as he awaited Emily's arrival but here, at the entrance to the harbour, it was becoming obvious that Sid's poetic vulgarity, coupled with Gerty's boisterous Can Canning, was proving to be not exactly the donkeys' idea of fun. In fact the beasts were finding the outrageous scenario to be so unsettling they were sailing close to the point of stampede.

'Clear orf!' or words to that effect, shouted the little old chap, swishing his cane ruthlessly at Sid. 'And especially you!' he growled, turning to Gerty as he threatened her with his cane. 'Go on, clear orf! Both o' yer!' he screamed at the pair of uncouth nuisances. And with that, the pair of uncouth nuisances did just that.

CHAPTER 8

I'M HALF CRAZY, ALL FOR THE LOVE OF YOU

Lifting herself from the cosiness of Mister Duvall's shoulder Emily stood to take a final view of the harbour before together, they commenced the short stroll from the promenade up the cliff top pathway, whilst ensuring they kept themselves out of sight and stayed well behind the Can Canning antics of Gerty and Sid's raucous, yet almost poetic, obscenities.

With Mister Duvall flirtatiously stealing the odd kiss or two, she was only too happy to encourage his playful hands to roam freely as they tickled her tummy at every opportunity. It therefore came as little surprise that his suggestion of them making use of the bench situated in front of the bandstand was taken up by Emily. Once seated Mister Duvall again welcomed her head to his shoulder but as they canoodled Emily chose to broach the subject of Sid's crudity.

'The song that Sid was singing, it's called *Ship Ahoy* she stated quite knowledgably.

'Oh really, well fancy that' he commented, sounding a little surprised.

'Oh yes, *Ship Ahoy* was always a firm favourite at family gatherings. Brother Bertie would be at the piano while the rest of us sang along to our hearts delight,' Emily sighed, relishing memories of a privileged childhood. 'But never have I heard it sung with such naughty words,' she giggled with an assumed air of disapproval.

Mister Duvall's opinion, however, was quite to the contrary.

'I can only assume that Sid's vulgarity came as a result of his overindulgence with that cursed alcohol,' he stated most disapprovingly.

It was then, like a bolt from the blue, that Emily asked the unexpected. 'So who on earth is Charlie boy?' never envisaging to be the recipient of a more half-soaked response.

'Do you know darling I seem to have spent all afternoon asking myself the very same question,' was his reply.

If Mister Duvall thought that such a flippant answer would satisfy the little lady's curiosity then he would have to think again as Emily pressed hard in search of some form of explanation.

'But I distinctly heard Gerty refer to you as Charlie boy, not once but twice,' she stated emphatically.

Another shrug of his shoulders indicated that as far as he was concerned the matter was closed and rendered irrelevant. 'I can only surmise that Mrs Skidmore was confusing me with her husband,' he suggested, yet still Emily was refusing to concede.

'But I definitely heard Sid refer to Gerty's husband as Billy and…' said Emily, suddenly distracted by the sight of the jacket laid across Mister Duvall's lap.

'And will you please just tell me, who does that jacket belong to?' she demanded to know, pointing a finger in exasperation at the said garment, and only the master of fib could respond with such a nonsensical reply.

'This jacket was gifted to me by my dear friend Max Miller,' an emotional Mister Duvall endeavoured to explain, stroking the garment as if it were a household pet. 'It was given in recognition of our long standing friendship and…' he would have said more but the quivering vibration of his lower lip was preventing him from doing so. That was until he threw his well honed skills of changing the flow of conversation into the mix.

'...And with regard to Mrs Skidmore referring to me as Charlie boy then again I can only blame Mrs Skidmore's excessive amount... amount of... aargh!' he screamed to the heavens as springing from his seat he went prancing around the bench, kicking out his leg every third or fourth skip in true hokey cokey fashion.

'Sorry about this darling,' he gasped, nearing completion of his second lap. 'It's the... aargh...I've got the cramp!'

Eventually a hopelessly out of breath Mister Duvall, collapsing back into his seat upon the bench, breathed a relevant question. 'Now where was I?'

'Aarh poor Lester, mommy's little soldier boy,' Emily mockingly teased as, cuddling him like a toy teddy bear, she planted a wet smacker of a kiss onto the side of his cheek.

Mister Duvall shook the suspect leg once more for luck. The ploy, the cramp attack that never was, had proved itself the perfect distraction.

With the bewitching hour of seven o'clock fast approaching it could mean only one thing, aunty's cocoa time. However Mister Duvall did feel, and understandably so, rebuffed when his offer of walking the lady to her door was abruptly dismissed.

'I think it best we say goodnight here,' Emily said in an obvious reference to her aunt's staunch views on the so called 'call up dodgers', a term which described the likes of Mister Lester Duvall to a tee.

Bringing her close for their goodnight kiss he felt compelled to ask 'Darling, we will be seeing each other tomorrow won't we?'

Emily pecked his cheek. The following day, she explained, being the last day of her holiday, would be taken up with preparation for her homeward journey, which entailed boarding the 7.30 am London train, but, as it was her intention to return to Mister Duvall's loving arms in a week or so, a small case would suffice.

'But I will be at the theatre tomorrow evening. That is of course if you want me there?' Emily giggled, delivering what was intended to be the evening's final kiss.

'Sleep well my darling,' Mister Duvall sighed, only for her to take him completely by surprise.

'I hope I sleep better than I did last night,' she tutted, sounding not at all best pleased. 'That rabble from the Spotted Dog was at it again, fighting in the street, shouting their foul language for everyone to hear, and all under my bedroom window.'

'Really?' gasped Mister Duvall in an award winning expression of disbelief. 'What time would this have been?'

'Oh it would have been past midnight,' recalled Emily. 'Most unacceptable but what can you expect from that downtrodden establishment?'

'Oh darling, how awful it must have been for you,' a sympathetic Mister Duvall sighed.

'But the skirmish must have woken you?' a surprised Emily queried, only for the gentleman of the theatre to respond pompously and totally unsympathetically, 'Sorry to disappoint darling but my room overlooks the backyard. As it happens I slept like a baby.'

'Well aren't you the lucky one,' Emily tutted as she removed herself from his arms. Picking up her picnic basket she delivered one last kiss to his cheek before moving away. Her kiss however, did not soften his hurt. Mister Lester Duvall, rogue, vagabond and master of the untruth was missing Miss Emily Bagshaw already. The only person he definitely wasn't missing was himself, Mister Charles Arthur Scrannage, formerly of the parish of Bethnal Green.

In the cool of the early evening sun, seated on the bench, alone with his thoughts, he found himself meandering down the highway of regret.

What if he'd have done the honourable thing and stayed with Maisy Gumbley? He would have become the proud father and provider for his offspring, a child who would now be aged around seventeen or eighteenish. Would he, or even she, have inherited the Scrannage gift of the gab? Sadly on this matter the gentleman of the theatre was destined to remain in ignorance for the rest of his natural days.

His thoughts then turned to the northern side of the Thames estuary, to the seaside resort of Southend upon Sea where he'd wasted more than enough of his precious time hiding from the ruthless Gumbley brothers. But wasn't it in Southend that a fellow pub crooner had informed him of the far superior rich pickings that lay in wait down on the south coast, at Brighton? It therefore begged the question; would this Dapper Dan of a character be seated here basking in the late afternoon sunshine, enjoying an uninterrupted sea view whilst dressed up to the nines in top quality schmutter? No, he most certainly would not. In fact if it hadn't been for the Maisy Gumbley episode this character would probably have remained a Bethnal Green loyalist whilst still answering to the name of Charlie Scrannage.

To add to this good fortune, Mister Lester Duvall was in the most enviable position of hovering on the brink of an intense relationship with a breathtakingly beautiful lady, who just happened to be not only six or seven years his junior but decidedly middle class, a far throw from the goodtime gals of Southend who, it had to be said, had been around the block a few times. Yes indeed his life was working out way beyond this son of Bethnal Green's wildest dreams.

A smug smile drifted across his face. For the princely sum of a pound a week this so called gentleman of the theatre was not only enjoying adequate accommodation for the duration of the summer, he also happened to be solely responsible for his landlady's nightly conjugals.

There was, however, a slight problem that was developing rapidly on the other side of the English Channel that could, if things didn't quite go his way, threaten to rock his dreamboat but, with the prospect of Emily spending the following week or so at brother Bertie's residence, it went without saying that next Sunday's roast beef dinner, washed down with a jug of the Spotted Dog's finest ale, and all courtesy of Gerty, would be found to be thoroughly acceptable.

Feeling the vale of golden slumbers becoming much too hard to resist, in full view of any passer by, Mister Duvall allowed himself to drift down into the sweetest of dreams.

One such passer by did not pass, choosing instead to stand motionless in front of the bench, depriving its dozing occupant of the setting sun's warm glow. Stirring uncomfortably, Mister Duvall opened his eyes and looked up to see a lone silhouette of a figure looming over him.

'Wake up sleepy head, its tea-time!' Emily chuckled playfully, waving her picnic basket into his face. 'Did you really think I'd let you have this beautiful sunset all to yourself?'

Shuffling along the bench in order to make space for his teatime spread, the gentleman felt a tad disappointed when the basket's content revealed itself to be merely a re-run of the earlier fodder, a couple of raspberry jam sandwiches, a few fruity biscuits and a replenished bottle of her aunt's homemade lemonade. However, with an over the top 'you really shouldn't have gone to all this trouble just for me darling', Mister Duvall complimented Emily by convincing the little lady that the spread was as welcome as springtime daffodils.

Resting her head upon his shoulder Emily could only look on as the gentleman of the theatre indulged himself in the delights of a turned up at the edge jam sandwich. A beaverlike gnawing session on a couple of fruity biscuits, accompanied by the sound of ecstatic sighing, was interpreted as the satisfying of intense hunger and a yearning for a sniff of the barmaid's apron would be quelled by the taking of generous sips of lemonade, if only Emily had remembered to bring a cup.

Always a gentleman and in accordance with hygienic etiquette Mister Duvall offered Emily the first swig and not in the least put out by this offer being declined he greedily gulped at the lemonade, drinking directly from the bottle.

His once bone dry tongue, now nicely lubricated, was then utilised by licking the spillage of jam from his fingers before wiping his mouth upon his shirt sleeve and for a moment he considered asking Emily to convey his heartfelt gratitude to her aunt, but then, in fear of repercussions, quickly nipped that idea in the bud.

Abandoning what remained of the jam smeared bread and the crumbs of broken fruity biscuits for the noisy gulls to devour, as she gave the tea towel a thoroughly good shaking Emily brought the towel to her nose and began to sniff inquisitively.

'Is there anything wrong my dear?' a concerned Mister Duvall asked.

'There's a rather unpleasant smell of fried eggs and bacon and I was wondering if, for some reason, it was coming from off this towel,' she replied as, continuing to sniff Emily shivered slightly.

'It really does go a little chilly as the sun sets,' said Emily, rubbing her hands together, and the gentleman of the theatre was quick to take the hint. Draping the double breasted brown jacket around her shoulders Mister Duvall welcomed the little lady into his arms, willing her to share with him the simplest form of relaxation.

Snuggling her head down upon his shoulder Emily, gazing out across the tranquillity of the English Channel, thought it appropriate to inform him of the latest news bulletin that she'd heard earlier.

'According to the BBC there are over one hundred and fifty thousand of our boys stranded at Dunkirk,' she sighed despairingly. 'Is this to be their final going down of the sun?'

Maintaining silence Mister Duvall took her hand and, with a little coaxing, the little lady collected up her picnic basket to accompany him on the short walk into Waterloo Street.

Taking Emily into his arms to whisper 'Goodnight sweetheart' softly into her ear, he once again indulged himself in the taste of her Regency Red lipstick before she took the handful of steps to her front door. Turning to blow a parting kiss it was then Emily realised that, with regard to her feelings for Mister Lester Duvall, gentleman of the theatre, that, just like the stranded British troops, she herself was nearing the point of surrender.

CHAPTER 9

THE END OF ME OL' CIGAR!

Striding across Waterloo Street, with the jacket slung casually over his arm, Mister Duvall, on hearing Sid's dulcet tones ringing loud and clear from the bar of the Spotted Dog, couldn't help but break into a chuckle.

'All the nice girls love a candle,' sang Sid launching into yet another rendition of his wickedly crude interpretation of *Ship Ahoy* and Mister Duvall quite understandably assumed that Gerty would be alongside of him, performing her knees up routine for all the great unwashed of Thanet to enjoy.

Skipping up the four steps to the front door of number 65 he turned his key in the lock. Stepping inside the hallway Mister Duvall immediately realised that he had assumed wrongly.

Alerted by the sound of gentle snoring the gentleman of the theatre sneaked a peep around the half open parlour door to be met with the sight of a sleeping Gerty. Sprawled awkwardly across an armchair, legs akimbo, his initial thought was to lift Gerty's head a little, slip a cushion beneath it and then, hoping not to wake her, lay the jacket over her. However it had been a long day and boy oh boy did he need a drop of the hard stuff.

Creeping along the gloomy hallway, on entry into the darkness of the kitchen it became apparent that his search for the Holy Grail would require a guiding light to spirit him along the path of righteousness to where hopefully a half bottle of gin would await his pleasure.

Fearful that switching on the kitchen's electric light bulb would awaken Gerty, a recollection of the previous evening reminded him of the two tapered candles, seated firmly in their respective saucers sited at either end of the top of the sideboard.

Working on the assumption that a box of matches would hold permanent residence on the side of Gerty's oven a fumble in the dark proved this assumption to be correct and fortunately the very first strike of the very first match resulted in a positive flame being applied to the wicks of the candles, sending rays of light dancing around the kitchen.

By juggling the two handles on the sideboard's top drawer, with a touch of gentle determination, to his surprise the drawer slid open with comparative ease hopefully to enable his fingers to root out Gerty's half bottle of the fiery stuff. Sadly, when his fingers got there the cupboard was bare, save for the messy ball of tangled cotton, a plentiful hoard of buttons, safety pins and hairgrips. Presuming Gerty had discarded the empty half bottle before surrendering herself into his welcoming arms the previous evening.

Unperturbed, Mister Duvall carefully slid the top drawer closed. Turning his attention to the second drawer down he found that also solidly crammed with unnecessary junk. In sheer frustration he slid it closed, only this time not so quietly. Third time lucky perhaps?

It was not to be and so, faced with a scorecard of three down and one to go, the gentleman of the theatre graciously accepted the fact that he was in the Last Chance saloon, which, in this case would be the bottom drawer of the sideboard.

Knees bent and employing the concentration of a safecracker, Mister Duvall noisily juggled with the bottom drawer's two flimsy handles until perseverance paid off. Waggling the drawer to and fro the damned thing finally slid open. Franticly delving his hand into the unknown he was initially rewarded with a couple of musty hand towels and an even mustier table cloth but the moment a tear trickled down his cheek was the moment his fingers stroked the shape of not a half, but a fully sized, bottle of mother's ruin.

Joyously he tore at the seal and gulped down a mighty mouthful of jungle juice straight from the bottle. Wallowing in the vicious sting of the neat gin as it hit the back of his throat with such venom that it was comparable to that of gargling with broken glass, he concluded that yes, it really tasted that good.

Pouring an approximate three finger measure into an empty cup from the table - whether the cup was clean or not was irrelevant - with shoulders back, Mister Duvall brought the cup to his lips. Braced in readiness for the impending bliss, a guilty conscience began telling him that Gerty should be informed of his loyal and faithful intentions with Miss Emily Bagshaw. Any hanky panky that had taken place between he and Gerty would from now on be confined to history. Holding the cup in the air Mister Duvall toasted his newly found outlook with a gulp, a swallow and not too loud a burp.

Amongst a scattering of crumbs in the middle of the table lay the bread knife and the remains of the loaf that had received such a hacking during breakfast. The whining and rumbling sound of his stomach was enough for his eyes to fall upon the pantry door situated just outside the kitchen, tucked beneath the stairs. Perhaps he possessed the psychic gift but instinct was telling him that the pantry's interior would more than likely resemble the tomb of Tutankhamen. Nevertheless, as he rose from his chair to succumb to temptation, a hauntingly ghostly voice spoke.

'I see you found the emergency supply then,' croaked Gerty, shuffling into the glow of candlelight.

'Care for a drop?' asked a somewhat startled Mister Duvall, offering up the bottle only for Gerty to ask 'Are you comin' up or what?'

Taking a leaf from the Book of Life which stated that a stiff one has no conscience, the gentleman of the theatre drained his cup of its content and mumbled to Gerty that one more shot of nectar would not go amiss. Juggling with the bottle, as Mister Duvall poured his last shot of the evening into his cup he realised that Gerty was no longer there.

Adopting a waste not want not policy he downed the nightcap in one greedy swallow, rose from the chair and readied for duty. Wetting the tips of his fingers with his tongue he doused the two candles on the sideboard and ascended the stairs. That roast beef dinner was beginning to smell good already.

At the top of the stairs, with all the panache of a downtown dance hall gigolo, he glided over the landing's urinal green coloured linoleum and entered Gerty's boudoir to be met with the sight of a sleeping head protruding from beneath the blanket.

Clumsily he began hopping from one foot to another as he somehow managed to shred, along with his socks, the white tennis pumps from his feet. Over his head went the sleeveless pullover whilst the irritating pressure on his shoulders was relieved by the release of the taut bracers, thus allowing the Oxford Bags to fall gracefully to the ground around his ankles. His grubby underpants were soon destined to travel the same route, granting his sweaty testicles the fresh air they had been craving all afternoon. Jerking the shirt up over his head he dropped the thing on the heap with the rest of the stuff. Picking up the mass of discarded clobber in one mighty scoop, he hurled the whole lot toward the corner of the room where, more by luck than judgement, the bundle landed upon the bucket-styled wicker chair.

Now naked as nature intended, Mister Duvall lifted the blanket and sidled into bed, settling beside the sleeping Gerty. With his head resting upon the pillow a feeling of contentment began to overwhelm him. Not only were the prospects for next Sunday's roast beef looking good, easing his troubled mind was the fact that no longer would he have to endure any more voyages aboard the Thanet Lady, but time would tell the tale.

'Mornin' Charlie boy' a voice croaked in little more than a muffled whisper and with her head now resting upon Mister Duvall's bared chest Gerty would be the one to initiate the clumsy cuddling that quickly morphed into what can only be described as an *every man for himself* groping session. Spurned on by the sound of Gerty's *oohing and aarhing*, the gentleman of the theatre was not too far behind her and gaining by the second but, as Mister Duvall contemplated entering the final furlong, Gerty's utterances suddenly ceased.

Lifting her head up to go eye to eye with him Gerty asked quite forthrightly. 'Charlie, did we get up to anything last night?'

'Of course we did,' replied a smiling Mister Duvall, stroking her hair.

A meaningful kiss to the nape of her neck caused Gerty to swoon in ecstasy and, turning onto his side, he once again demonstrated his expertise in such sensuous activity. Manoeuvring his body into a position whereby his *bits* dangled freely against Gerty's thigh, Mister Duvall knew only too well, from times spent with the wickedly wild forbidden fruit of both Southend and Brighton, not to mention Maisy Gumbley, that this course of action would be guaranteed to incite plenty more heartfelt *oohing and aarhing* from the lady. In the firm belief that Gerty was fast becoming hotter than a Red Indian's backside, Mister Duvall's next move was to apply his tried and tested technique of nibbling at the lady's earlobe whilst his exploratory fingers slowly ventured south. At the appropriate moment, his fingers would be replaced by his lips.

Surfacing for air, however, the gentleman of the theatre was to discover that there would be no more *oohing and aarhing*. His efforts had all been in vain. Gerty had fallen fast asleep.

Apparently Mister Duvall must have followed suit because he suddenly became aware of a bleary eyed Gerty hovering at the side of the bed and looking absolutely dreadful.

''Ands orf cocks and on with socks,' she gasped.

Staggering toward the bedroom door, without even turning to look at him, Gerty mumbled. 'It's gone eleven, do yer want yer breakfast or don't yer?'

It was easier said than done but Mister Duvall scrambled out of bed to make use of what space remained in the chamber pot, the wicker chair over in the corner being his next port of call.

Surprisingly the freshly crumpled white shirt went on him a lot easier than it came off and with no problems to report concerning the underpants and Oxford Bags, after a brief period of contemplation, during which he managed to match one of the socks with its identical twin, he decided to wear the Bags without the aid of its bracers. A quick once over in the dressing table mirror suggested that he had been dragged through a hedge backwards but nevertheless Mister Duvall, putting vanity and Gerty's nagging aside, descended the stairs to enter the kitchen where a well hung-over Gerty was sprucing up her face and general appearance with the help of the sideboard's mirror. Turning to acknowledge Mister Duvall's presence she nodded to the table where a plate with a fried egg, two rashers of bacon plus a doorstep of buttered crusty bread awaited his attention.

Once seated at the table, lifting the teapot, he offered to play mother, only to be met with instant rejection.

'I ain't got time!' snapped Gerty. 'I should've been over the Spotted Dog 'alf hour ago.'

Shrugging his shoulders Mister Duvall, chomping merrily away, couldn't help but notice a large saucepan, near full to the brim with hot water, simmering on the gas stove.

'When you've filled yer boots you can give that Barnet *(Barnet Fair/hair)* o' yours a seein' to with that,' she said, pointing to the saucepan. 'You look like the wild man 'o Borneo.'

Running his fingers through the unkempt greasy mess on the top of his head Mister Duvall, whilst in agreement, returned himself to the matter of chomping.

'And while yer at it,' continued Gerty, 'you can give that mush o' yours a scrapin'' and picking up her wayward husband's shaving mug from the top of the sideboard she slammed it down on the table alongside his breakfast plate.

'Look at yer. Right ol' paraffin *(Paraffin lamp/tramp)* ain't yer,' Gerty sneered, spitting out insults whilst slipping on her raincoat to disappear down the hallway.

Any other man would have been deeply hurt by such comments but for the gentleman of the theatre it was simply water off a duck's back. However it would be a matter of seconds before Gerty returned.

'I'm sorry Charlie, I got a right thumper on me this mornin' an' I blame Sid. Loadin' me up with all that rum,' she moaned. 'A lamb to the bleedin' slaughter, that's what I was.'

Without raising his head Mister Duvall jabbed the corner of the rock hard crust of bread into his egg yolk to noisily bite into the crust.

Promising hand on heart that she would be putting the feelers out for a weekend chunk of beef Gerty paused for a couple of seconds before tossing an emotional spanner into the works.

'That's if we're still 'ere next Sunday,' she said, her voice now seemingly devoid of any form of humour.

'What do you mean, if we're still here?' mumbled Mister Duvall incoherently, struggling to free a knuckle of bacon that had wedged between his teeth.

'Like you said on the stage, our boys are all on their tod *(Tod Sloan/own)* an' up against all them Germans,' she stated, gesturing in an easterly direction towards the sea.

Finally freeing the wedged knuckle to plonk it down onto the rim of his plate Mister Duvall picked up the teapot to drain what was left into his cup before proceeding to say precisely nothing.

'Oh Charlie,' sighed Gerty in desperation. 'What are we gonna to do if the balloon goes up?'

Staring over the rim of his teacup Mister Duvall had no option but to respond. 'If anyone knows what he's doing, then it's Mister Churchill,' he sighed before seeing off what remained on his breakfast plate, save of course for the abandoned knuckle of bacon.

With Gerty gone the gentleman of the theatre turned to the task of cleansing his hair. Filling the brown crock kitchen sink with a mixture of cold tap water and half of the saucepan's steamy content he then returned the pan to the lowly flame on the stove. Picking up Gerty's empty cup from the table he lowered his head over the sink and scooped a cupful or two of the mixed water over his slimily greased thatch. Wincing a little with the heat of the water he had no choice but to continue with this soaking of his scalp before even thinking of the introduction of soap into the procedure.

Sliding the bar of carbolic from its berth upon the draining board, Mister Duvall worked up ample lather from the bar to then rub the stuff quite vigorously into his scalp. Unfortunately with the lather cascading down his forehead, causing his eyes to sting like hell, he blindly reached out across the draining board for the tea towel.

A wipe of his eyes with the said towel revealed that although there were signs of a fair amount of the sickly slimy grease floating around in the sink, a further exhilarating rinse would be required and result in the tea towel being wrapped around his head.

Taking Billy Skidmore's razor from the mug Mister Duvall waggled the blade wildly around in the sink's still warm water before waltzing over to the sideboard where, stooped at the knees, he aligned his face with the mirror. A few raw scrapes of the soapless razor rendered his chin soft as a newly born baby's backside. Aware that with the towel still wrapped around his head he bore an uncanny resemblance to the Sheik of Araby, Mister Duvall remained ultra confident that with his hair dried and coiffured, he would once again carry the look of a theatrical gentleman.

Unravelling the tea towel from around his head to return it to the draining board for further use, he purloined one of Gerty's combs from the sideboard's top drawer to again stoop and align his face with the mirror. Following a couple of failed efforts, the perfect slightly off centre parting to his damp hair was attained, but, as he admired his newly formed creation, Mister Lester Duvall found himself asking the very same question that Gerty had asked earlier.

'Just what are we gonna do if the balloon does go up?'

CHAPTER 10

SHADOWS MAY FALL ACROSS THE LAND AND SEA

Bursting with the breeziness expected from a gentleman of the theatre, on opening the front door of Number 65, Waterloo Street Mister Duvall soon realised why Gerty had opted for her raincoat. Weatherwise the world looked as depressingly dull as dishwater. His initial intent had been to clear the four steps down onto the pavement with one mighty leap but the donning of his dark grey gabardine raincoat put the kybosh on any such activity.

With grey clouds threatening and with him bearing an uncanny resemblance to the man from the Prudential Insurance Company, so Mister Lester Duvall, once down on the pavement, brusquely strode out along Waterloo Street in the direction of the bandstand. Presuming that Emily would be preparing for her following day's journey, as he passed Waterloo House, he offered not a single glance in her direction. Instead, to protect his recently degreased thatch from the elements, the gentleman of the theatre buried his head down into the upturned collar of his raincoat.

At the side of the bandstand the untidy heap of discarded deckchairs were indicating that an afternoon concert, courtesy of the brass band, had been cancelled. Not that it made the slightest difference to him and so, taking the cliff top pathway down to the harbour Mister Duvall was to encounter, apart from Gerty, his first sighting that day of a human being.

On the pavement, at his station directly outside the revolving doors of the Royal Hotel, dressed resplendently in a crimson frocked coat, that came complete with military looking paraphernalia and a pair of fancy gloves, stood the hotel's doorman. Unfortunately this dandy looking but rather elderly character was struggling to hold down the top hat perched upon his head to prevent it from being blown out to sea and all the way across to Dunkirk.

Other than that there was no other person to be seen, save for the cockles and whelks man who, it seemed, had lost the will to laugh.

What a contrast to twenty four hours earlier when, beneath the brilliance of the afternoon sun, the colourful sight of the small boats and cabin cruisers bobbing around in their moorings like fairground kewpie dolls had provided such joy to the down for the day brigade.

Today however would tell a different story. With the stiff sea breeze whipping in from off the English Channel, a three worded notice, chalked upon on the not too big blackboard positioned at the harbour entrance read *No sailings today* which quite accurately summed up the day's weather prospects, although history would proudly record that sailings did recommence the following morning.

With an independent air Mister Duvall marched along the promenade to where the not over-small fairground was situated. Twenty four hours previously it had played host to hundreds of folks and families as they indulged in the thrills and spills of the fair, but sadly not today. All the stalls were boarded up and the various rides were covered over by ugly grey canvas tarpaulins that flapped around irritatingly in an unforgiving wind.

On the beach, beneath a battered trilby, alongside his four weary donkeys, was the little old chap and it would be an impossible task to ascertain who looked the most bored out of the five of them.

Having Mister Duvall down as a potential rodeo rider the old chap looked over to him and nodded towards the donkeys but, taking into consideration the strenuous antics of the night before that he'd been subjected to, the gentleman of the theatre had good reason to decline the invitation.

Turning his back on the old chap, he retraced his steps back to the harbour where he found that the cockles and whelks man had upped stumps and taken his barrow with him, unlike the Royal Hotel's doorman. A soldier to the end, that elderly gentleman had, with undying loyalty, managed to keep a tight hold of his top hat.

On the clifftop, as he neared the bandstand, Mister Duvall paused to take in what was a thoroughly depressing view, nothing like the resort's promotional posters that adorned the walls of the booking hall and the platforms of the town's railway station in which scantily dressed young ladies were portrayed playing beach ball on the sun-kissed sands.

Re-entering Waterloo Street Mister Duvall slowed his pace in the hope of catching the slightest glimpse of Emily but even this little ray of sunshine was denied him. Stepping back into Number 65 the gentleman of the theatre hung up his raincoat to ascend the stairs for the purpose of an afternoon siesta in what had been his original first floor room.

Collapsing onto the single bed, Mister Duvall began psyching himself in readiness for his evening performance. Although he hadn't set foot into this room for the past couple of days it was apparent that Gerty hadn't either for there, still on the table, untouched by human hand, was his Saturday evening bread and pickles supper. To a gentleman of theatrical persuasion the temptation of an afternoon snack was hard to resist, but resist he did as, with eyes narrowing, he drifted into the land of nod.

After what felt like the briefest of catnaps Mister Duvall suddenly sat bolt upright. Hurling the blanket to one side his instinct was telling him to look over to the corner table. The bread and pickles supper had mysteriously disappeared but, over the back of the dining chair hung his pair of shiny at the rear black flannels along with what had been his crumpled white shirt. A spirited examination of the flannels and shirt revealed that both had been subjected to Gerty's hot iron.

He was also more than happy to be reacquainted with his pair of black shoes, now gleaming with shininess. A close inspection of the leather, however, revealed that the newly acquired cleansing was probably down to a manic session of spit and polish.

A vigorous thrashing of cold water into his face followed by the vibrating of his pursed lips into the hand towel was then encored by a quite unique gargled rendition of *Men of Harlech*.

And so, now clad in his newly pressed flannels and shirt, not to mention his shiny footwear, Mister Lester Duvall, gentleman of the theatre, was able to render himself fit for purpose.

His walk to the theatre that early evening was as miserable as Hell and it came as little surprise to not see a soul, save for three or four die hard folk intent on taking the early evening air. Unfortunately they were walking in the opposite direction.

The dark grey clouds had begun releasing their drizzly content as Mister Duvall sought to reacquaint himself with the wording of his rousing speech in regard to the stranded British troops but, as he looked to the English Channel for inspiration, all there was to be seen was a heavy sea mist that was refusing to budge.

The stage door clock was showing twenty minutes to showtime and with Sid nowhere to be seen Mister Duvall headed directly to his dressing room. Removing the candy striped blazer from the nail on the back of the door he replaced it with his gabardine raincoat but, slipping into the blazer, he started to get the feeling that something wasn't quite right. There didn't seem to be much of a buzz around the place. In fact the only sound to be heard was the muffled murmuring of voices filtering through from the Topsy Turvys' dressing room. However, with showtime looming, the gentleman of the theatre simply got on with the job in hand.

First up was his habitual warm up - a soft shoe shuffle around the room which would conclude with a full rotation of his body. A knock on the door brought him to an abrupt halt.

Without waiting for the invitation to come in Sid, dressed in his frayed at the lapels monkey suit and looking like death warmed up, barged in.

'You look a worried man Sid,' commented Mister Duvall. 'Nothing to do with your stint in the Spotted Dog last night I hope.'

Sid, however, had far more important things to discuss.

'We're on for a very poor 'ouse tonight,' he said, failing to conceal the grounds for his troubles which left Mister Duvall with no option but to ask, 'Just how poor are we talking?'

'We've only got maybe a dozen or so in,' sighed a woeful Sid. 'It's all lookin' a bit 'Umpty Dumpty to be honest. There just ain't anybody about an' it might 'ave somethin' to do with what's goin' on over at Dunkirk.'

Mister Duvall eased down into the wobbly wicker chair as Sid stated prophetically. 'You mark my words sir we'll soon 'ave 'em back. They'll be queuin' from 'ere all the way down to the bandstand this time next week.'

Reaching up Mister Duvall patted the back of Sid's hand in gratitude only for Sid to add a few more comforting words.

'An' if you 'ave to take a drop in yer rocks *(Rocks of ages/wages)* don't get worryin'. My 'alf a crown a week will be adjusted accordin'ly.'

Satisfied that the gentleman of the theatre was now fully informed Sid hobbled out of the dressing room and into the backstage area to somehow find the necessary inner strength needed to holler out his obligatory pre-show announcement of 'Five minutes to showtime!'

From out of the wobbly wicker chair the gentleman of the theatre rose. With a flick of the wrist, from the blazer's top pocket popped his dickie bow to find itself secured around his neck in all but a matter of seconds. Casually plonking the straw boater down onto his recently cleansed head of hair the boater came to rest exactly as it was supposed to, hanging cheekily over the brow of his forehead.

His timing could not have been nearer perfect. As if on cue the hopelessly out of tune piano struck up, willing the gentleman of the theatre to go soft shoe shuffling out of his dressing room and into the backstage area. Meeting the Topsy Turvys face to face a couple of whispered hellos and polite smiles were exchanged but Mister Duvall was a happy man, having arrived in time to see Sid make his entrance.

Basking in all the adulation that a dozen or so people could generate Sid, disguising his hangover so beautifully, exclaimed 'Welcome to our summer variety show Postcards from the Seaside!' before leaning through the footlights to ask the dozen folks seated in front of him ''Ave any o' you visited that nudist camp just outside o' Margate yet?

Although met with a negative response Sid was not deterred.

'Yeah they opened a nudist camp last August an' our King an' Queen popped down to cut the ribbon an' declare the place open.'

Being now well and truly hooked, the audience, sparse as it was, found they were hanging onto Sid's every word as he continued to lead them down the path of naughtiness.

'So as the Lord Mayor o' Margate was showin' 'em round this nudist camp the Queen thought she recognised the bloke sellin' the ice cream an' asked the Lord Mayor 'isn't that Dick Brown?'

'Yes your majesty,' the Lord Mayor replied, 'we've 'ad a marvellous summer!'

With the theatre reeling in hysterics, Sid stepped back through the footlights, allowing the laughter to recede before grandly announcing 'Ladies and gentlemen, at great expense, I give you the Topsy Turvys!'

Bounding from out of the wings the two little ladies commenced to reel off their corny as hell patter that the dozen or so folks had paid their hard earned shillings to hear as Sid, slowly descending the four wooden steps and still suffering from the after effects of the previous day's overindulgence, muttered a *never again*, solemn vow to himself before delivering the news to Mister Duvall that he was yearning to hear. Emily was in attendance.

'She's four rows back, in the aisle seat, and lookin' fit as a butcher's dog,' said Sid, pursing his lips and clenching his fist to wistfully sigh. 'Ooh if only I was twenty years younger.'

The gentleman of the theatre however had opted to ignore Sid's manic fantasies, preferring to concentrate on whatever old hat jokes the Topsy Turvys were putting over.

'I say, I say, I say' said Topsy.

'Yes, what is it now?' asked Turvy, sounding pretty fed up with the whole procedure leaving Topsy to continue with their silly nonsensical conversation.

'I'm getting the plane out tomorrow,' Topsy stated proudly to the audience.

'And are you going to fly over Germany and give Adolph Hitler a right old pasting?' inquired Turvy, punching the air with exaggerated aggression.

'No, I'm shaving half an inch off the back door!' was Topsy's absurd reply that had the sparse the audience howling in hysterics.

Guessing that his introduction was nigh Mister Duvall took to the first of the wooden steps up to the wings only for Sid to grab him by the arm. 'So what was I supposed to be gettin' up to in the Spotted Dog last night then?' he warily enquired

'Treating everybody to a very saucy rendition of *Ship Ahoy* answered Mister Duvall as he struggled to free himself.

'An' I s'pose Gerty was doin' 'er Can Can bit,' tutted Sid. 'She normally does when she's 'ad a few.'

'Not at all, while you were Ship Ahoying it Gerty was in her parlour tucked up nicely and fast asleep. Now if you don't mind?' insisted Mister Duvall, yanking his arm from out of Sid's clutches, only for Sid to quickly grab a further hold, having decided to take the gentleman of the theatre into his confidence.

'Keep this to yerself but if it wasn't for all that rum I put away I might 'ave 'ad me wicked way with Gerty,' sighed Sid, sounding wrist slashingly suicidal only to find an unsympathetic Mister Duvall's priorities lay elsewhere as the Topsy Turvys launched into their well rehearsed, albeit obligatory, introduction for him.

'Ladies and gentlemen,' they proclaimed in nigh on perfect unison 'it is our pleasure to welcome onto the stage, coming directly from the Brighton Hippodrome, where he has appeared, on so many occasions, alongside the one and only Max Miller…'

Although this over the top approach was making little impression on their audience the Topsy Turvys soldiered on, determined to build on the intensity of their words.

'This gentleman has actually sung on the wireless with Billy Cotton!'

At long last a reactionary gasp came from the stalls was enough to spur the two Pierroted clowns to even more excitability. 'Yes he's here, here with us, on the Isle of Thanet, not only for tonight, but for the entire summer season! Ladies and gentlemen, it's the man himself, Mister Lester Duvall!'

The striking up of the hopelessly out of tune piano literally begged Mister Duvall to soft shoe shuffle himself onto the stage and into the limelight. Performing his 360 degree body swivel complete with the shimmering of hands and fingers soon saw the gentleman of the theatre off and running as taking a Topsy Turvy on each of his arms he commenced to glide the pair of them effortlessly around the stage.

Four rows back, in the aisle seat, just as Sid had said, sat an enthralled little lady who was about to become even more enthralled as Mister Duvall, beginning his song, slipped a cheeky wink in her direction.

He sends her postcards from the seaside, warm greetings and beside
Crossed kisses he wishes she were there.
He'd take her promenading and then be serenading
Her on the swing boats at the fair.
Those kisses he'd be stealing would send her heart a reeling
As the brass band played oompah on the pier

As he sang he was visualizing holding Emily in his arms twenty-four hours previously when, from the deck of Thanet Lady, they had shared the view of the fairground as it played host to the array of the 'down for the day' folks, not forgetting their sheer joy at marching playfully around the harbour's quayside to the oompahing sound of the brass band.

With his eyes now fixed on Emily, as his face transmitted the broadest of grins in her direction Mister Duvall lifted the straw boater from his head to begin waving it high above his head as he brought his song to a resounding climax.

Postcards from the seaside, warm greetings and beside
Postcards from the seaside, wish you were here!

Thin on the ground as they were, Mister Duvall bowed to acknowledge his audience before pausing until the applause was reduced to all but silence. By now psyched into preacherman mode so the gentleman of the theatre crossed his fingers and hoped that the words he was about to deliver would find their way to the hearts of each and everyone seated before him. Steadying himself he inhaled deeply, convincing himself that his diction would be heard with the utmost of clarity and Mister Lester Duvall began his speech.

'Ladies and gentlemen I'm sure there is no need to remind you that, as I speak, our brave boys are just twenty odd miles or so across the Channel.'

With his confidence growing and satisfied with a 'so far so good' state of play, he endeavoured to elevate his audience to the next level.

'Our boys, brave boys, preparing to meet the might of the German army!' he fervently stated when suddenly the well of his memory ran dry.

'Our boys… our boys… our boys,' he kept repeating as an uneasy unrest began to filter around his sparse audience.

Attempting to buy himself time Mister Duvall glanced sideways to the wings in the hope of some form of prompt but, with his mind now playing unpleasant trickeries the sarcastic piece of advice he had received from Sid on that first morning had returned with vengeance and had begun to ring around unmercifully inside of his head.

'Keep on the move and they'll never nail you,' had been Sid's below the belt jibe, suggesting that he, Mister Lester Duvall, was nothing more than a cowardly conscription dodger.

In sheer panic Mister Duvall looked to Emily but no sooner had his eyes found hers so those stinging words 'You shouldn't be here, you should be over there doing your bit,' that Emily had laid at his door were back to haunt him.

With those acidic words eating ravenously into his guilt ridden soul, as Mister Lester Duvall, gentleman of the theatre, prepared himself for the ultimate humiliation, so Lady Luck smiled down on him.

As if it were a heaven-sent miracle the audience, all twelve of them, Emily included, began to believe that the sweat seeping from Mister Duvall's brow had been induced by patriotic emotion and he suddenly found himself in a position to pick up from where he'd left off. Raising a clenched fist, with threatening aggression, Mister Lester Duvall, with the fire now ablaze in his belly, recommenced.

'Our boys, yes our boys, fighting like lions for their King and for their country,' he stated proudly as with all the spirit he could muster, he hammered home the message to everyone present that all was not lost.

'And so ladies and gentlemen,' he continued, 'tonight, as we drift into golden slumbers let us join in mutual prayer. Indeed let us pray, even at this late hour, for the safe return of each and every one of our brave boys! Let us bring the boys home soon!'

Bucketfuls of phoney sincerity, like wedding confetti, went swishing around the auditorium as that hopelessly out of tune piano began coaxing a marching rhythm from its nicotine stained ivories and, with the sight of the Topsy Turvys moving militarily either side of him it would prove to be his most rousing performance to date.

Let's bring the boys home soon. Let's hope the next full moon
Sees all the fighting done with Gerry on the run
And Hitler sinking faster than a lead balloon

It was purely a matter of time for the audience, all twelve to be up on their feet, showing their highly charged loyalty by clapping along to the stirring marching beat as, flanked by the Topsy Turvys, the gentleman of the theatre brought the song to a spiritually fulfilling finale.

Home fires will always burn until their safe return
Boys so boldly brave they risk an early grave, marching to
our nation's tune
Into the fires of Hell, God bless and keep them well
Let's bring the boys home soon!

The ovation that Mister Duvall received was quite unprecedented. Bringing himself to attention, he grandly saluted before being commanded by the Topsy Turvys to 'left turn and quick march!' leaving his audience, in true showbiz tradition, begging for more.

However the moment he arrived in the wings was the moment Mister Duvall applied the necessary sharp tug to his bow tie and crammed it into the top pocket of his blazer.

In the sanctuary of his dressing room, seating himself comfortably into the corner wicker chair, the gentleman of theatre, just for a few moments, simply allowed the rest of the world to roll by. And that was when the wobbly legs of the wicker chair slowly creaked and collapsed. Without as much as a by-your-leave.

CHAPTER 11

AFTER THE DANCERS' LEAVING, AFTER THE STARS ARE GONE

Like a sheik in his harem Sid knew exactly what he was there for but hadn't a clue where to start as, with notebook and pencil in hand, he was pondering how on earth he could skim a few shillings off the top of this financial disaster for himself when a tapping on the stage door interrupted his fraudulent train of thought. Opening the door Sid was met by the sight of a small black umbrella hovering above a grey raincoat.

'Hello Sid,' said a friendly voice which Sid recognised immediately as belonging to Emily.

'Come on in darlin'!' he said joyfully. 'Mister Duvall should be along in a minute.'

'They say it's bad luck to have your brolly open indoors,' said a superstitious Emily as fiddling with the clip on the shaft of the brolly she stepped inside.

'Well things can't get any worse,' Sid sighed to himself as he closed his notebook and wedged the pencil behind his ear.

'Oh Sid, I want you to know I enjoyed every minute of yesterday,' said Emily, sneaking a peck to his cheek as Sid gently brought the palm of his hand up to his forehead.

'Ooh my loaf *(Loaf of bread/head)*,' he moaned. 'Was I in a bit o' soap *(Soap and bubble/trouble)* this mornin'?'

'You poor poor man,' said a sympathetic Emily, not having the faintest idea what he was talking about. 'But you do know I'm leaving tomorrow,' she added, only to be pleasantly interrupted by the arrival of the gentleman of the theatre.

'And you will be back with us in a week or so, won't you darling,' said Mister Duvall, cheekily stealing a kiss as Emily began gushing with praise for him.

'Lester, you were just so wonderful this evening. Everyone simply loved you,' she enthused, returning his kiss.

'Oh they loved 'im alright, all twelve of 'em,' Sid mumbled, opening the stage door in order for the happy couple to vacate.

'Aha but I've a bone to pick with you Mister Lester Duvall,' giggled Emily, 'You didn't tell the joke about your grandfather falling into the beer and drowning.'

'That my dear was because it was total one off and strictly for the landladies,' Mister Duvall snootily answered, continuing to edge towards the door, only for Sid to steal a little thunder from him.

'Well accordin' to Billy Skidmore, it was 'is granddad what fell into the toe nail *(Toe nail/ale)*,' he said as, still holding the stage door open Sid then suggested that they, Gerty included, celebrate Emily's eventual return to their fold by way of all of them repeating the Thanet Lady experience with another trip around the bay.

The very thought of his precious thatch being once again exposed to the blustery elements of the English Channel sent horrific shivers down Mister Duvall's spine. Would he, a highly reputable gentleman of the theatre, be prepared to plaster his hair again with the greasy scrapings from the bottom of Gerty's frying pan? No, he most definitely would not!

Stepping out onto the cliff top pathway, with the two lovebirds jostling for space beneath Emily's tiny brolly, Sid stopped to slam the stage door tightly shut. 'Mister Duvall sir, don't be late tomorrow night!' he called out into the darkness.

Mister Lester Duvall had no intention of being late. In fact, though he did not yet know it, the morrow would see him performing on a far grander stage, and to a guaranteed full house.

Sharing the umbrella 70/30 in Emily's favour, his recently cleansed hair now dampened by the evening's drizzle, Mister Duvall, in keeping with the ways of a gentleman, engaged in schmaltzy chit chat with his lady-love who, by way of pitching the silliest of questions his way, was becoming more starstruck by the minute.

Asking if it were possible to be introduced to Billy Cotton Emily received a most positive response from him.

'Of course my darling, I'm sure Mister Cotton would be only too happy to make your acquaintance. In fact I'll see to it next time I'm at the BBC,' Mister Duvall replied, digging a rather large hole for himself.

Strolling towards the bandstand, with nary a thought for consequence, Mister Duvall continued to spill even more fairytale bilge as he spoke of his plans for the future which would include appearances at the Brighton Hippodrome, some of them alongside his dear friend Max Miller. Swirling his arms Mister Duvall prophesied that very soon, once Mister Hitler had been put to bed, the promenades of the south coast would once again be illuminating the night skies with the doors of all their highly prestigious theatres once again open for business. Suddenly that rather large hole was in danger of becoming a crater from which he would never clamber, and yet, crazy as they were, these absurd statements would seal Emily's forever kind of love for him.

Approaching their favoured bench Emily assumed that, soaking wet as it was, the said bench would be the ideal venue for their temporary farewell kissing and cuddling session to take place. Mister Duvall however had other ideas.

Escorting the little lady up the marbled steps to the centre of the bandstand neither was surprised to discover they had the entire place to themselves.

Being the gentleman, Mister Duvall took the brolly from Emily's hand and collapsed it before dropping it to the floor. Bringing himself to attention he then formally requested 'Miss Bagshaw, may I have the pleasure of this dance?'

'But we have no music,' sighed Emily.

That was to be no impediment. Placing his arms around her, and with the little lady's head resting upon his shoulder, the gentleman of the theatre began to croon softly into her ear.

He sends her postcards from the seaside, warm greetings and beside
Crossed kisses he wishes she were there.

The fragrance of her California Poppy was having its usual effect, igniting the flame of desire within him as they commenced to sway to the song's romantic rhythm. Moving in closer, his fingers fiddled with the buckle on Emily's raincoat until, progressing to the coat's front buttons, he had opened her raincoat, so his hands could delve inside to lovingly embrace her.

Tonight, or so it would seem, Mister Duvall's advances were being met with little, if any, resistance. With her fingers rummaging through his hair, Emily's lips granted him permission to sample the wondrous flavour of her Regency Red lipstick, a taste that, when enhanced by the sweet fragrance of her perfume, would be guaranteed to drive any hot-blooded man to the point of insanity. And after all, a gentleman of the theatre is only human.

He'd take her promenading and then be serenading
Her on the swingboats at the fair

Sensing that her surrender was nigh Mister Duvall glided his fingers slowly over the contours of her tiny breasts to be confronted yet again by those dreaded tortoise shell buttons.

The first button, as did the second, opened easily and, spurred on by the enthusiasm of Emily's kiss, his hand moved to her partly exposed breast. Everything in the garden was looking swimmingly rosy as Mister Duvall's interpretation of a slower than slow foxtrot went into a highly sensual wind down.

Those kisses he'd be stealing would send her heart a reeling
As the brass band played oompah on the pier
Postcards from the seaside, warm greetings and beside
Postcards from the seaside wish you were here.

And on that sad and sorry note his world came crashing down.

'Lester, please no. Please Lester, stop it,' Emily urged, frantically pushing him away and Mister Duvall, disappointed to say the least, was left to gasp, 'But darling…'

Despite her quivering fingers Emily managed to re-fasten the two top tortoise shell buttons on the front of her blouse but as she struggled with the raincoat's belt buckle the lady offered a saving grace. 'Give me a little time,' she whispered, returning herself willingly to his arms.

Mister Duvall picked up the umbrella from the floor. Juggling with the release clip until the tiny brolly sprang open, he handed the umbrella back to her as if nothing untoward had ever happened.

Linking arms they descended the marble steps of the bandstand to walk across the road and into Waterloo Street. They were but ten yards or so from Waterloo House when Emily suddenly halted in her tracks.

'Lester, look, the Spotted Dog…it's closed,' she gasped in astonishment and the little lady was indeed correct for there was the pub, silent as the grave and in total darkness.

'At least I'll get a good night's sleep,' Emily mused as her head found its way onto Mister Duvall's shoulder. 'Oh Lester I really don't want to leave tomorrow,' she sighed.

With the prospect of a roast beef Sunday lunch rolling through his mind Mister Duvall said little to discourage her. Instead, with Emily in his arms, the gentleman of the theatre chose to once again smother himself with the taste of her Regency Red lipstick before whispering 'Goodnight sweetheart, I'll see you in my dreams' into her ear.

Willing herself away from him Emily made it as far as the front door of Waterloo House until, after a momentary hesitation, she was back in his arms.

'I'm going to remember this evening for a long, long time,' she sobbed, never realising that every moment of the evening would remain in her memory for the rest of her days.

At the front door of Waterloo House, Emily turned and forced a smile. One final blow of a kiss and she stepped inside. Farewell is a lonely sound.

The unwritten law of romance is to never look back but the gentleman of the theatre did just that. Turning to gaze at the pillared circular shrine that only a few minutes previously had served as their makeshift love nest and was now such a cold and desolate place Mister Duvall was convinced that any form of relationship with Gerty must be terminated forthwith. He tucked his head down into the collar of his raincoat, and ambled his way across Waterloo Street. Like a condemned prisoner en route to the gallows he mounted the four steps up to the front door of number 65 and placed his key into its lock.

Pausing, he looked over his shoulder to the soulless Spotted Dog. The night before had seen the place as a hive of jollity for all the local rogues and vagabonds merrily knees upping to Sid's lewd but rib tickling rendition of *Ship Ahoy*, and yet tonight, for some unexplained reason, the place bore the look of an abandoned saloon in some tumble-weeded Wild West cowboy town.

For him, Mister Lester Duvall, gentleman of the theatre, the time had come to face the music. Turning the key he eased the door open and stepped inside.

At the kitchen table, in the glow of candlelight, Gerty sat awaiting his presence. With clumps of her black curly hair protruding from beneath her flowery turban and her hands clutched at a bottle of gin as if it were a crystal ball, had it not been for her grubby pinafore, Gerty could have easily passed herself off as an end of the pier fortune teller.

'Take yer mack orf and sit down,' she said, gesturing to the dining chair on the opposite side of the table and, with Gerty's wish being his every command, Mister Duvall dutifully obeyed.

Pouring him a healthy measure of firewater from the bottle into an empty teacup and lolling back into her chair Gerty patiently waited for Mister Duvall to open proceedings.

'The audience was a little thin on the ground tonight,' he blithered, taking his first sip of the evening. 'Rather peculiar don't you think?'

'Not really,' Gerty replied, sounding as if she couldn't care less. 'There is a war goin' on you know, or 'adn't you noticed?'

A period of awkward silence followed until Mister Duvall happened to mention that the Spotted Dog was closed.

'No, you've that wrong Charlie boy,' she snapped, shaking her head. 'It ain't even ten o' clock yet.'

Seeing no reason to pursue the forced conversation any further the gentleman of the theatre returned to his mother's ruin.

Again an awkward silence prevailed until a question, intended to start the ball rolling, was pitched by Gerty. 'Said your goodbyes to 'er ladyship then?' she asked rather warily, peering over the rim of her gin-filled teacup.

With no response forthcoming Gerty, acting upon impulse, grabbed the tea towel from the draining board and tossed it across the table to where it landed in his lap.

'Try wipin' your barnet *(Barnet fair/hair)* with that' she suggested in exasperation.

Standing to vigorously rub the tea towel into his hair, once satisfied that any excess drizzly stuff had been removed, Mister Duvall slung it back onto the draining board.

Sitting back down into his chair he then gulped a mouthful of gin, smacked his lips and, looking Gerty square into her face, began to spell out his plans for the foreseeable future.

'I'm sorry Gerty but whatever there was between us is finished,' was his opening statement, delivered in a firm and proper manner.

With no response from the other side of the table, he continued. 'Miss Bagshaw will be returning here in a week or so,' the gentleman of the theatre, patting his ruffled hair down flat to his scalp, stated but a rude interruption from Gerty was to completely derail him.

'So, where's 'er ladyship gone orf to then?' she queried, her eyes narrowing suspiciously.

With a pre-rehearsed reply tucked nicely up his sleeve, the gentleman of the theatre's response simply oozed utmost confidence.

'Emily has returned to the family residence in order to care for brother Bertie,' was his reply and one which resulted in Gerty, who found the whole scenario preposterous, bursting into a fit of the giggles.

'I gotta be honest, Charlie boy,' she chuckled, 'I ain't ever 'eard that one before,' and the more Gerty giggled the more Mister Duvall became an unhappy bunny.

'That is what Miss Bagshaw told me and I believe her,' he snapped. 'Brother Bertie did his bit at the Somme and Emily, being the kind and caring lady that she is, looks after him.'

'An' all credit to 'er,' proclaimed Gerty sarcastically, raising her cup to propose a toast. 'Let's drink to 'er ladyship!' she grandly suggested and with Mister Duvall responding with appropriate etiquette, all seemed quiet on the Western front.

However the peace was soon to be rattled by Gerty lobbing another of her verbal grenades into the mix, one that would completely wrong-foot him. 'So where is 'ome for 'er Ladyship?' she enquired with a whiff of the caustic.

'Well it's...it's er...it's er...you know,' Mister Duvall mumbled as, lost for words, he began pointing anywhere and everywhere but in no particular direction.

'No, I don't know, so tell me,' Gerty urged. 'Come on Charlie boy I'm all ears.'

Unfortunately all he could offer was the vaguest of replies.

'Well...it would be...probably, yes it's er... it's 'er,' he stammered, snapping his fingers in frustration whilst presenting Gerty with the opportunity to bury him alive.

''Ow's Mayfair, or even Park Lane sound? Or Buckin'am bleedin' Palace for that matter!' she roared, angrily smacking the table with the palm of her hand. 'The truth is Charlie boy you ain't got the faintest idea where she lives! You don't know the first thing about this woman do yer!'

'I know Miss Bagshaw to be a fine and well-connected lady,' stated Mister Duvall. 'Listen Gerty, you're a proper Bethnal Green, good time gal, I'll give you that,' he said in an effort to come across as a fine and caring person 'but you have to admit that Miss Bagshaw is pure class.'

That comment, delivered with all the warmth of a landlord's heart, ensured Mister Lester Duvall, gentleman of the theatre, would not remain upright in his chair for very long.

'Who the bleedin' 'ell do er fink you are!' screamed Gerty at him as, like a volcano, her temper erupted. 'Tellin' me I ain't got clarss!' she bawled and no matter how hard he tried to shoehorn in any form of apology there was no way Mister Duvall could quell Gerty's raging anger.

'This is my 'ouse!' she screamed. 'An' talkin' of 'ouses, I'll tell you this Charlie Scrannage, don't think you and yer fancy piece is shackin' up 'ere,' hollered Gerty, stretching herself over the table to jab a stern finger into his face ''cause you ain't!'

An uncomfortable few moments of eyeball to eyeball was only halted by a reaction from Mister Duvall that came dripping with toffeed nosery.

'I would imagine that Emily and I will be moving into Waterloo House where we will be boarded quite generously by her elderly aunt,' he said, smarmily leaning back into his chair.

A shake of the head accompanied by a sigh of disbelief from Gerty should have prepared him for the verbal dagger that was about to be plunged into his highly inflated ego.

'I'll tell yer this for nothin' Charlie boy - I've lived facin' that there 'ouse for nigh on sixteen years, an' I ain't never, not once, in all them sixteen years, seen any sign o' life comin' from inside the place. So either the biter's got bit or the ol' gal's frew a seven,' was how Gerty summarised Mister Duvall's intended domestic arrangements.

'An' as for all this lah dih dah Mister Lester Duvall, gentleman o' the featre malarkey, 'ow long will it be before this fancy piece o' yours sees through it all,' she growled mercilessly. You rubbin' shoulders with the likes o' Billy Cotton an' Max Miller - I ask yer?'

Placing his elbows down onto the table Mister Duvall dropped his head into his hands.

'Without Mister Lester Duvall I have no Emily,' he mumbled through shaking fingers to add. 'And without Emily I have nothing.'

Shocked, deeply hurt but not completely unsurprised Gerty sneaked her hand lovingly across the table.

'You got me Charlie,' she whispered as, taking his hand into hers, she allowed her emotions to show. 'I'm 'ere for yer. I know this place ain't up to much but you can still do yer singin' in the summer.'

'Oh Gerty,' Mister Duvall sighed despairingly as he lifted his head. 'You haven't been listening to a word I've said have you?'

Never a truer word was spoken.

'This war ain't gonna last forever Charlie. Winston will sort it all out, you'll see,' Gerty gabbled. 'I've even got yer a piece o' beef for Sunday an'…'

Sadly she was fooling no one but herself as the sheer unhappiness of the situation overwhelmed her.

Offering little in the way of consolation Mister Duvall sat silently staring at the floor until Gerty, bringing her grubby pinafore up to her face, wiped her eyes to make the sudden announcement that she was sick and tired of the whole damned affair.

'But I will give yer one final piece of advice, Charlie Scrannage,' she said as, rising from the chair. Jabbing her finger more or less into his face Gerty growled. 'Stick to yer own kind, Charlie. Yer can't carry on livin' a lie forever? There, that's it, I'm orf to bed,' she concluded.

On top of the sideboard was a plate covered by a saucepan lid. Removing the lid she plonked the plate down onto the table before taking one of the saucers that contained a lighted candle from off the sideboard and managed to make it as far as the kitchen door.

'If you feel lonely in the night you know where I am,' were her final words before disappearing into the darkness of the hallway.

On the plate was a crust of buttered bread, a not too badly sized lump of cheese and a fair portion of mango chutney, all his for the taking.

Refreshing his cup with a drop of gin for what would be his final slug of the evening, Mister Duvall picked up the crust. Attempting a bite he immediately took the decision to abort, the crust being as solid as a cricket ball, leaving him with just the cheese and mango chutney to toy with.

Having successfully scraped a furry substance off the rest of the pickle, he set about coating the cheese with what remained of this culinary creation to demolish the lot in two good mouthfuls. Shoving the plate to one side the gentleman of the theatre then drained his cup of mother's ruin to bring his supper to an end with a hearty belch.

Picking up the remaining saucer and candle from the sideboard Mister Duvall met the challenge of the wooden hill that would lead him to Bedfordshire face on. His intention had been to veer into his own hardly used room but instead his feet chose to continue his ascent to the summit, where, in half expectation, Gerty lay.

No words were necessary. Mister Duvall stripped, wet the tips of his fingers and doused his candle. Guided by the moon light, he sneaked beneath the blanket and cuddled up to Gerty.

'I'm sorry about yer supper Charlie,' she whispered as she rested her head upon his chest. 'It's 'ard gettin' anythin' decent with all this rationin'.'

'That's alright Gerty, I wasn't that hungry anyway,' sighed Mister Duvall, putting his arm around her coinciding with a noisy rumbling of his stomach.

'I did manage to get us a bit o' beef for the weekend though,' she said, lifting her head to kiss his cheek, only for Mister Duvall to mockingly yawn, 'Goodnight Gerty,' into the darkness.

A minute or so later Gerty lifted her head from his chest and sat bolt upright.

'I can't believe the Spotted Dog 'as closed early,' she gasped 'I 'ope there's nothin' goin' on.'

CHAPTER 12

I'LL BE LOOKING AT THE MOON AND I'LL BE SEEING YOU

It would have been around 7 o'clock the following morning when, from across the street, the sound of a front door being pulled shut alerted a dozing Mister Duvall to sleepily surmise that the sound of clacking shoes upon the pavement was down to Emily. Closing his eyes to return himself to a state of unconscious the gentleman of the theatre was then reawakened by Gerty raucously hollering from the bottom of the stairs.

'Charlie, Charlie, get down 'ere quick!' she was shouting and sensing immediately that things weren't quite as they should be, the predictable '''ands off cocks an' on with socks' wake up call being missing, Mister Duvall roused and crawled out of the bed.

A scoop of cold water from the wash basin into his face induced a sudden gasp to the heavens that was suppressed by the spluttering of his lips into a nearby hand towel, yet still Gerty continued to holler 'Charlie, Charlie get down 'ere quick!'

Having pulled on his basics the gentleman of the theatre descended the stairs. Wondering what all the fuss was about, tucking his shirt down into his trousers, Mister Duvall sauntered into the kitchen.

'There's somethin' goin' on down the 'arbour an' I don't like it one bit,' said an irritated and wound up Gerty, sliding a fried egg from out of the pan for it to land onto his plate alongside a shrivelled rasher of bacon. 'I ain't jokin' Charlie boy, somethin''s wrong. I can feel it in me water.'

'How do you mean, something's wrong?' queried Mister Duvall, his eyes scanning the table for any sign of bread, regardless of condition.

'Can't you 'ear it?' Gerty asked, picking up the teapot. 'Just listen to it, down the 'arbour, all that shoutin' an' bawlin'. An' them fog 'orns blastin' out,' she tutted, pouring him a cup of tea.

In dismissive mood, as he took his seat Mister Duvall suggested that the commotion might well be down to a sailing regatta or something similar but Gerty remained unconvinced. Rattling her knuckles on the table in frustration she again spat out her concerns when suddenly those concerns were brought to prominence by frantic banging on the front door.

'Gerty, Gerty, open the door! Open the door Gerty!' Sid was screaming through the letterbox.

'Alright, alright, I can 'ear yer,' she yelled back, heading down the hallway, but, on opening her front door so Sid, like a man possessed, went barging straight past her.

'Where's Mister Duvall! I gotta see Mister Duvall!' he was bawling as, rushing into the kitchen Sid collapsed breathlessly against the sideboard.

'You'll be 'avin' one o' your funny turns if you ain't careful. Now just sit yerself down an' 'ave a cup o' tea,' Gerty advised but Sid, ignoring the advice, instead turned his attention to Mister Duvall to produce two keys from his fist.

'You'll need these for tonight,' Sid panted, holding up the larger key of the two. 'This one opens the front doors to let the wagons *(Wagon shunters/punters)* in an' this other one is for the stage door. Now put 'em in yer Lucy *(Lucy Lockett/pocket)* an' don't lose 'em.'

Taken completely by surprise the gentleman of the theatre rose from his chair. Licking the egg yolk from his fingers

Mister Duvall obeyed Sid's instructions to the word. Pocketing the two keys into his trousers he, along with Gerty, could only stand open-mouthed as an out of breath Sid continued with an explanation of exactly what was occurring.

'I'm sailin' *Fanet Lady* over to Dunkirk along with all the other blokes what's got boats. Gerry's got Dunkirk surrounded an' some'ow we gotta get Tommy orf them beaches,' Sid gasped before a spontaneous idea arrived from out of thin air.

'You don't fancy comin' with us do yer mate?' asked Sid, turning to Mister Duvall.

Gerty was quick off the mark to instantly wag a threatening finger into Mister Duvall's face. 'Don't you even think about it Charlie boy. You're goin' nowhere,' she more or less commanded but those chilling words of hers prompted Sid to flippantly remark.

'Blimey if I didn't know any better I'd say there was somethin' goin' on between you pair,' before issuing an invitation that would be extremely hard for the gentleman of the theatre to wriggle out of.

'Any bloke what ain't got a boat is more than welcome to put in with us.'

The strongest hint possible had been dropped but sadly ignored and so, with an uncomfortable silence abounding, Sid had little choice but to call the gentleman's bluff.

'So 'ow about you then Mister la di da Lester Duvall?' he sarcastically asked. 'Will you be practicin' what you preach?'

With no response forthcoming, sensing what he believed to be an overpowering stench of cowardice, Sid's tone of voice grew angrier by the second.

'Every bloke, every able bodied bloke is puttin' in with us,' he snarled in frustration 'but not you. So I will ask you one last time, 'ow about you?'

As if in shame the gentleman of the theatre lowered his head momentarily before lifting it back up to speak the words that Sid was expecting and Gerty was dreading.

'Alright Sid, I'm coming with you. Gerty would you kindly pass me my raincoat?' he requested, holding out his hand in anticipation.

'Oh no you don't Charlie Scrannage, you ain't droppin' me like an 'ot tater!' she retorted, giving the table an almighty thump.

And that was when the penny finally dropped with Sid.

'So there is somethin' goin' on between you pair,' he mumbled in bewilderment, scratching his balding pate. 'An' who's this Charlie Scrannage bloke when 'e'es about?'

'Leave it Sid, I'll tell yer later,' a panicking Gerty snapped as she tried frantically to avoid any possible confrontation, only for Sid to respond extremely nastily.

'Leave it? I ain't leavin' nuffin',' he growled, pointing a finger at Mister Duvall. 'You know I got lovin' feelin's for Gerty!' he yelled. But then along comes you with all yer poncey ways!'

Swinging an arm back Sid delivered a stinging slap across Mister Duvall's face. 'What's the matter, ain't one woman good enough for yer!' he hollered in temper.

Gerty immediately jumped into the middle of the two men, but Sid, fired with rage, shoved her out of his way to raise his clenched fists menacingly at Mister Duvall.

'Come on fight me! Fight me, yer two-faced bastard!' he shouted and, with the gentleman of the theatre remaining silent and motionless, he instinctively laid another slap on the gentleman's reddening cheek.

'Just pack it in, Sid. You're way out of your depth,' warned Mister Duvall, maintaining his composure, but Sid was refusing to listen.

'Me? Out o' my depth?' he mockingly asked, letting fly with a punch that landed squarely on Mister Duvall's chin, causing the gentleman of the theatre to rock back on his heels.

Like the victorious prize fighter he truly believed himself to be, a jigging Sid began waving his mitts in the air to enthuse 'Look at 'im Gerty! 'E's as yella as custard!'

However, as Sid riding a surging wave of confidence, swung another punch in the direction of Mister Duvall's jaw, he was to find this attempt easily parried.

'For the last time, pack it in,' a riled Mister Duvall told him in no uncertain terms but Sid, still refusing to listen, was to learn the hard way the perils of living in a fool's paradise.

'Didn't I tell yer Gerty? 'E's just a yella bellied coward,' Sid chuckled as he attempted yet another strike. Not only was this one easily parried but Mister Duvall, faced with an exposed stomach, took full advantage of being gifted an open goal and, without breaking sweat, he delivered a simple jab to Sid's tummy, taking the wind out of the poor chap's sails.

Stupidly thinking this would put an end to the matter Mister Duvall relaxed his guard only for Sid, his pride badly wounded, to lunge at him.

In retaliation Mister Duvall grabbed Sid by the scruff of his shirt collar and yanked him up so viciously that his feet actually left the ground.

'Don't 'it 'im Charlie!' Gerty screamed. 'Please don't 'it 'im!' and, luckily for Sid, the gentleman of the theatre did as requested. Casting the poor fellow aside, albeit with considerable force, Sid went bouncing off the table to crash into the sideboard and slide slowly down to the kitchen floor, where, in a heap, he came to rest.

Filled with remorse Mister Duvall rushed to his side but was immediately rebuffed.

'Leave me alone,' a badly shaken Sid groaned, although he did allow Gerty to help him up and into a chair.

Massaging his winded stomach, Sid managed to gasp. ''E got me smack in the Derby *(Derby Kelly/ belly)*,' before nodding over at Mister Duvall. 'Who is this man Gerty, an' what's 'e to you?' he asked but it would be the gentleman of the theatre who supplied the answer.

'It's true, Gerty and I are old friends but that's all there is to it. We're friends, that's all. Emily is the only woman for me,' but Sid didn't seem remotely convinced or now even interested.

'I gotta get meself down the 'arbour some'ow,' he muttered, struggling out of the chair and back onto his feet.

'You're a good man Sid and you deserve a better man alongside you,' Mister Duvall called out. 'But I'm still coming with you.'

'You can't leave me Charlie, not like this,' Gerty sobbed, burying her head in her hands but Mister Duvall had little choice.

Gently patting her shoulder, he sighed. 'I'm sorry Gerty but Sid's right, the time has come to practice what I've been preaching.'

Gerty made a final plea for Mister Duvall to turn the other cheek but it was no use.

'It's like you told me last night, I can't go on living a lie,' said a remorseful Mister Duvall before addressing Sid in the most formal of manner. 'When all this is over Sid, if you still want to sort me out, then we'll do it the East End way, out in the street and with fists,' but Sid's only concern remained the matter in hand.

'Fanet Lady will be sailin' for Dunkirk in twenty minutes, with or without yer,' he muttered as, still nursing a winded stomach, he hobbled out of the house en route for the harbour.

Mister Duvall lifted his raincoat down from the rack and lovingly embraced Gerty. 'Don't worry, I'll be back,' he vowed and, with a kiss to her cheek, Mister Lester Duvall, gentleman of the theatre, was gone.

Alone at the kitchen table, drowning in her own sorrow, as she sat pondering the choice to either sink or swim, it dawned upon Gerty that her services as cleaner-cum-barmaid would be required at the Spotted Dog and, being a woman of substance, she chose to swim.

Abandoning all thoughts of a tidy up following the recent kafuffle, once into her coat, and with the racket down at the harbour becoming noisier by the minute, Gerty strode across Waterloo Street where she found, much to her annoyance, the door of the Spotted Dog to be locked and bolted. A couple of demanding thumps on the door however resulted in the landlord's missus putting in a rare appearance.

'We're shut and there's nobody 'ere. They've all gone orf to Dunkirk,' stated the missus before rudely slamming the door closed a hell of a lot quicker than she had opened it.

On the pavement of a deserted Waterloo Street Gerty looked beyond the bandstand, to where she observed a fair few spectators who had gathered on the clifftop pathway. Within two minutes she had taken her place amongst them.

At the harbour entrance Mister Duvall was met by the manic sight and the raucous noise of absolute chaos with men running here, there and everywhere, barking instructions to anyone who was minded to listen whilst others were taking to their small boats in preparation for a mission that could, at best, be described as perilous.

Hurrying determinedly over the quayside cobbles an undaunted Mister Duvall caught sight of Sid hovered over a capstan frantically trying to untangle Thanet Lady's mooring ropes.

'Okay Sid, I'll see to that,' stated a confident Mister Duvall as he approached. 'See if you can get the motor started?'

For a second or two a wary Sid hesitated before casting his fate to the wind.

'I'll need a lift up from yer,' he replied and immediately Mister Duvall, grabbing the poor chap from behind, with a swift heave ho, hoisted the poor chap into the air to go gambolling over the side of Thanet Lady. Crawling on his hands and knees across the deck, Sid, by making use of the cabin cruiser's wheel, was then able to bring himself up and onto his feet to commence the firing up of the good Lady's motor. Accompanied by the customary profanities and with a prayer to the heavens, three or four of turns of the key resulted in the grinding sound of metal filtering up from below deck. The fruity language of Sid's plea to the Almighty turned into joyous exclamation as, from out of the good Lady's rear, blew enough thick black smoke to enable Sid to steer Thanet Lady from her berth and into action.

Only forty-eight hours previously Mister Duvall had publicly stated that his and the good Lady's paths would never cross again and yet, here he was, standing proudly upon her deck as every craft in the harbour, regardless of size, began slipping their moorings, honking their foghorns to noisily broadcast that *England expects every man to do his duty.*

Like colliding fairground dodgems the small boats went bumping and bouncing into one another in their efforts to clear the confines of the harbour and there, at the heart of it all, was Sid, unfortunately causing a tiny motor boat, not much bigger than your average rowing boat, to very nearly upturn by steering Thanet Lady smack into the tiny boat's side. As its lone occupant struggled to steady his teeny weeny craft in the swell, Mister Duvall had no option but to offer the most humble of apologies to the cockles and whelks man.

Once clear of the harbour each of the small craft amalgamated on the flanks of an ever-growing flotilla bound for the beaches of Dunkirk, to where the seemingly hopeless task of rescuing three hundred thousand stranded British troops from the jaws of Hell awaited their attendance.

Up on the clifftop pathway Gerty, along with all the other onlookers, was waving frantically at the boats, sending out messages of undying love when suddenly, as it encountered a heavy cloud of rolling sea mist, the flotilla disappeared from sight.

CHAPTER 13

'TIL OUR HEARTS TELL US WHEN TO SING AGAIN

'There you go Sid, pour yerself a nice cup o' tea,' said Gerty, placing a freshly made pot down onto the kitchen table.

'I don't want nothin' thanks,' muttered Sid morosely.

Unperturbed Gerty suggested a light supper. 'There's some cold beef in the pantry,' only to be met with yet more negativity.

'Maybe there's somethin' on the wireless,' she sighed, but Sid's response was pretty blunt.

'Only Billy Cotton,' he replied.

'In that case we might as well save the battery,' Gerty snapped in frustration when an unexpected knock on the front door, be it for better or worse, injected a spark of life into the early evening's proceedings.

'You stay right there Sidney, we can't have you overdoin' it,' said Gerty in her normal sarcastic tone as, rising from her chair, she disappeared down the hallway. A few seconds later Sid heard Gerty's voice calling out to him. 'Sid its Emily, Emily's 'ere!'

Looking up to see Emily entering the kitchen Sid allowed a smile to return to his face.

''Ello darlin', pull up a floorboard for yerself,' he said, nodding towards Gerty's vacant chair. 'Pour the gal a cup o' tea, Gerty,' he suggested and Gerty did exactly that.

Placing her small suitcase down on the floor beside her Emily came straight to the point.

'Sid I've just been to the theatre but it's in darkness,' she said, sounding a little concerned.

'There's no show tonight, darlin',' Sid sighed, reaching for Emily's hand, 'and there won't be one for a very long time.'

'But where is Lester?' asked a bewildered Emily, breaking into panic mode. 'We've fallen in love. Lester and I, we're going to spend the rest of our lives together.'

Laying a comforting hand upon Emily's shoulder, Gerty looked to Sid. 'It's best you tell 'er,' she said.

'Tell me, tell me what?' begged Emily as Sid prepared himself to be the bearer of the saddest of news.

'It was a week ago, the day you went 'ome,' Sid began. 'Me and Mister Duvall, we set out aboard Fanet Lady to sail across the Channel with all the other boats.'

'Oh my god,' Emily gasped in horror, bringing her hands up to her face. 'Not Dunkirk. Please, dear god, tell me it's not Dunkirk,' she pleaded as Sid continued.

'I've never seen nothin' like it in my life. There they were, just boys, paddlin' around in the water or waitin' on the beaches to wade out to us in the boats, an' every five minutes there'd be a couple o' German planes swoopin' over, firin' their machine guns all over the place. I tell yer, some of our blokes copped it terrible.'

His voice now cracking and with his eyes welling, Sid paused to console himself.

'Go on Sid, give yerself a good blow,' Gerty said, taking a hanky from up her sleeve and Sid, blowing hard into it, offered the hanky back to Gerty who kindly told him to 'keep it for later', thus allowing Sid to continue.

'Me an' Mister Duvall was 'angin' over the side o' the boat, pullin' up anybody we could out the water,' sniffed Sid. 'I said to Mister Duvall 'we gotta get out of 'ere quick, we're full up as it is,' but there was a lad, only a nipper, stuck in the water an' was 'e in some trouble 'cause 'is kitbag kept pullin' 'im under. Before I knew what was 'appenin'. Mister Duvall jumped into the sea an' went swimmin' over to the lad. 'E yanked the kid up by 'is 'air an' dragged 'im an' the kitbag over to Fanet Lady an' me.'

Beginning to weep uncontrollably Sid paused before once again wiping away his tears to continue to relive the nightmarish events.

'That's when I saw the plane comin',' he sobbed grasping Emily's hand. 'I 'oisted the lad onto the deck double quick but Mister Duvall was strugglin' to climb back up the side o' the boat. I leaned over to 'elp 'im but the plane was 'eadin' straight for us. As I was pullin' Mister Duvall back onto the boat was when the bullets started zippin' through the water thick an' 'eavy.'

With his hands covering his face, Sid spurted out the words Emily had been dreading.

'I was 'oldin' onto Mister Duvall as the bullets ripped into 'is back an' 'e started screamin' unmerciful.'

'It's alright Sid,' whispered Emily, 'you can stop now,' but Sid, still weeping heavily, was determined to soldier on.

'All of a sudden Mister Duvall stopped screamin'. I looked into 'is mincers *(Mince pies/eyes)* but they'd glazed over an' I knew there and then that I 'ad to let 'im go. Mister Duvall fell back into the sea an' just went floatin' away. There was nothin' I could do. The poor bloke was dead anyway.'

A short period of silence followed before Sid lifted is head. 'But I did bring sixteen of our boys back 'ome. Most of 'em in a bit of a two an' eight *(Two and eight/state)*, an' would you believe, I still managed to clout the quayside,' he croaked through his tears.

'So Lester did his bit then?' Emily asked, still holding Sid's hand tightly.

'Oh yeah 'e done 'is bit alright' sobbed Sid. 'Mister Lester Duvall, a true gentleman o' the featre done 'is bit.'

'And he was only thirty years of age,' Emily sighed lovingly as she pushed her untouched cup of tea away towards the middle of the table.

'Thirty? No age is it,' commented Gerty, smoothing the back of her head whilst flexing her shoulders. 'Not that I knew 'im that well. 'E was just a bloke what come knockin' on my door a couple o' weeks ago.'

Sid, taken aback by Gerty's little white lie, chose to keep quiet whilst Emily put what she truly believed to be an appropriate suggestion into the mix. 'I think Billy Cotton and Max Miller should be informed,' she said. 'I'll make contact with the BBC.'

'Its best you leave all that to me darlin',' said Gerty in a comforting tone as Emily, picking up her small suitcase, rose from the chair. Pecking Sid's cheek with a farewell kiss she then turned to give Gerty much the same.

Making it as far as the hallway, having fought so hard to contain her emotions, Emily surrendered to the inevitable and broke down in floods of tears.

Now cradled by Gerty she cried and cried until the little lady could weep no more, and it would be an apparently composed Emily who corrected the seating of the tiny straw hat upon her blonde hair, whereupon she felt able to once again face the world.

Gerty, now joined on the doorstep by Sid, could only stand and watch as, with her small case in hand, Emily walked away, never once to look back over her shoulder. Even Waterloo House did not warrant so much as a glance but she did pause, just for a few moments, at the bandstand, as she did at the bench, to reflect on the events of that evening a week or so ago when she almost, but not quite, gave herself intimately to Mister Duvall.

Arriving at the harbour entrance Emily observed the small boats aplenty as they bobbed around in their moorings, noting that none were sporting colourful bunting, appearing instead in a somewhat battle scarred state.

However it would be sight of a dozen or so badly wounded troops, obviously late arrivals from Dunkirk that willed her to listen to her heart.

Sadly there would be no more oomparring from the brass band for these soldiers to march along to as they staggered proudly over the cobbles on the quayside. Even the cockles and whelks' man was noticeable by his absence but, there again he may have made, as had Mister Duvall along with many others, the ultimate sacrifice.

Blowing a kiss out to the other side of the English Channel Emily turned away from the harbour and headed for the railway station.

'I reckon we could both do with some fresh air,' said Gerty and, much to her surprise, Sid agreed. Arm in arm they strolled to the top of Waterloo Street, crossed the road and manoeuvred themselves around the heap of deckchairs that were piled alongside the bandstand. Taking seats upon the bench, Sid bided his time before venturing an arm around Gerty's shoulder.

Like a pair of first date young canoodlers on the back row of the local picture house, as if they were staring at the silver screen, together they sat, gazing out to sea.

'If only I'd 'ave kept my big mouth shut 'e'd still be 'ere,' a remorseful Sid sighed as a respectful Gerty managed to maintain her silence for all of half a dozen seconds.

'Like 'e told yer, we knew each other from back in Befnal Green, but it was a long time ago and there was nothin' in it in the first place,' she said with more than an air of sadness before concluding, 'There, I said me piece an' I don't wanna 'ear no more about it.'

Looking to her left she then nodded towards the theatre. 'But I would like 'is striped blazer an' straw boater for keepsakes,' Gerty sighed. 'I 'spose 'is clobber is still 'angin' up in 'is dressin' room.'

'Give us a week or two an' I'll see what I can so,' an uneasy Sid replied, removing his arm from around Gerty's shoulder.

However that response alone would be enough to lift Gerty's spirit. Rising to her feet she asked. 'Fancy a drink Sid? I know the Spotted Dog's got some beer on. I saw the dray wagon drop a couple o' barrels orf this mornin'.'

Sid stood up from the bench. Giving his wonky leg a couple of shakes to get his blood back into circulation he commenced to escort the lady to their favoured watering hole.

'So where's this Charlie Scrannage bloke figure in all o' this?' Sid timidly asked, taking Gerty to within spitting distance of slight annoyance.

'I've just told yer, I don't want to 'ear no more about it,' she snapped when Sid, as the Spotted Dog loomed into view, suddenly brought himself to an abrupt halt.

'Gawd blimey,' he exclaimed, smacking his forehead with the palm of his hand, 'I give the featre keys to Mister Duvall! The keys to the featre, they're still in Mister Duvall's pocket!'

The theatre remained closed for seven years, reopening its doors in mid-June of 1947 when a new theatre replaced the old one which had been damaged beyond repair during a bombing raid. No candy-striped blazer nor straw boater were ever recovered.

At the railway station Emily walked determinedly through the booking hall and onto the platform from where the London bound train was about to depart. Directly in front of her was an open carriage door, and stepping aboard, she found herself standing alone in the buffet car. Her timing could not have been more perfect. The guard immediately blew his whistle and slammed the door shut firmly behind her.

The wheels of the train had actually begun turning when the carriage door flew open and a soldier, his head heavily bandaged, came scrambling in. The bandage was really quite bloody but Emily, being the lady that she was, looked elsewhere, giving the impression that she was finding the Kent countryside far more fascinating. She didn't even hear the request for 'Tickets please' coming from the approaching elderly, uniformed gentleman.

'May I see your ticket madam?' the elderly gentleman politely asked.

'Oh yes, of course,' a flustered Emily replied, forgetting for a moment that she hadn't actually bought a ticket as she was still in the throes of emotional upheaval. Trying as best she could to explain that having travelled down earlier in the day but sadly on a one-way ticket, she found herself overwhelmed by the predicament she was in.

'Don't worry, it will be our little secret,' whispered the elderly collector, slyly winking his eye before moving along the buffet car to where the bandaged soldier stood.

'How's your opponent lookin' then?' the ticket collector playfully joked only to find the soldier to be presently devoid of humour.

'What's your name son?' the elderly gentleman asked warmly to which the soldier, in typical military manner, barked 'Private Skidmore, sir!'

'So Private Skidmore,' the collector enquired, 'what do your pals call you?'

'Me mates call me Billy an' I ain't got a ticket. All I wanna do is get 'ome.'

'And where would home be for you Billy?' asked the uniformed gentleman, to which the soldier, eyes front and shoulders back, sharply replied, 'Befnal Green, sir!'

The ticket collector smiled. 'Will St. Pancras do?' he asked light-heartedly before, not even waiting for a response from the soldier, he shuffled himself out of the buffet car and into the corridor of the next carriage to resume his 'Tickets please' routine.

With rural Kent now behind her and the view from the buffet car window becoming more urbanised, Emily, still clutching her small case, began to prepare for the bustle of central London but with the train now slowing so the sound of the rhythmical pattern of its wheels seemed to be somewhat reminiscent of Mister Duvall's song, spurring her to softly sing the lyrics to herself as she inwardly prayed that her whispering voice would find a way to him.

He sends her postcards from the seaside, warm greetings and beside
Crossed kisses she wishes he were there.

Closing her eyes Emily recalled that first morning on the pathway outside of the stage door when, by a simple twist of fate, she and Mister Duvall had first met quite by accident, bumping into one another and of how she had been spirited inside the theatre by Sid to witness Mister Duvall soft-shoe shuffling across the stage to perform his song for her and for her alone.

He'd take here promenading and then be serenading

In her mind she revisited the Sunday afternoon they'd spent together on the deck of Thanet Lady and of how, as he'd held her tenderly in his arms, so the view of the beach and the fairground had been enhanced by Mister Duvall's singing.

Her on the swingboats at the fair
Those kisses he'd be stealing would send her heart a reeling
As the brass band played oompah on the pier

With its wheels now reduced to no more than a sauntering pace so the screeching of its brakes, followed by the obligatory jolt, brought the train to a shuddering stop.

Postcards from the seaside, warm greetings and beside

But Mister Lester Duvall would not be here and, with that thought in mind, Emily realised that her journey was over. She would not be returning to the Isle of Thanet.

With the knowledge that memories last longer than dreams, Emily opened her eyes. Glancing to her left she noticed that the carriage door was wide open. The soldier had obviously disembarked but as she contemplated the precarious step down from the buffet car onto the platform she was met with the sight of a helping hand being raised.

Grasping the hand quite firmly Emily was surprised to see that this offer of assistance was coming from the soldier but, in attempting the step down she tripped and stumbled, collapsing into his arms.

Apologising most profusely for her clumsiness she became aware that the bandaged soldier was sniffing outrageously, be it in a comical manner.

'Smells like California Poppy to me,' Private Skidmore chuckled, removing his hands from around her waist to allow the little lady the luxury of juggling the tiny straw hat head back into place upon her head.

With the soldier crying out the message of 'Be lucky', Miss Emily Bagshaw, spinster of the parish of who knows where, smoothed her flowing grey skirt, turned away and simply vanished, as if by magic, into the swirling mist of engine steam.

Postcards from the seaside, wish you were here.

FICTION FROM APS BOOKS
(www.andrewsparke.com)

Davey J Ashfield: *Footsteps On The Teign*
Davey J Ashfield *Contracting With The Devil*
Davey J Ashfield*: A Turkey And One More Easter Egg*
Davey J Ashfield*: Relentless Misery*
Fenella Bass: *Hornbeams*
Fenella Bass:: *Shadows*
Fenella Bass*: Darkness*
HR Beasley*: Nothing Left To Hide*
Lee Benson: *So You Want To Own An Art Gallery*
Lee Benson: *Where's Your Art gallery Now?*
Lee Benson*: Now You're The Artist...Deal With It*
Lee Benson: *No Naked Walls*
TF Byrne *Damage Limitation*
Nargis Darby: *A Different Shade Of Love*
J.W.Darcy: *Ladybird Ladybird*
Milton Godfrey: *The Danger In Being Afraid*
Jean Harvey: *Pandemic*
Michel Henri: *Mister Penny Whistle*
Michel Henri*: The Death Of The Duchess Of Grasmere*
Michel Henri: *Abducted By Faerie*
Hugh Lupus *An Extra Knot (Parts I-VI)*
Ian Meacheam: *An Inspector Called*
Ian Meacheam: *Time And The Consequences*
Peter Raposo: *dUst*
Peter Raposo: *The Illusion Of Movement*
Peter Raposo: *Second Life*
Peter Raposo: *Pussy Foot*
Peter Raposo: *This Is Not The End*
Peter Raposo*: Talk Of Proust*
Tony Rowland: *Traitor Lodger German Spy*
Andrew Sparke: *Abuse Cocaine & Soft Furnishings*
Andrew Sparke*: Copper Trance & Motorways*
Phil Thompson: *Momentary Lapses In Concentration*
Paul C. Walsh: *A Place Between The Mountains*
Paul C. Walsh*: Hallowed Turf*
Michael White*: Life Unfinished*

Printed in Poland
by Amazon Fulfillment
Poland Sp. z o.o., Wrocław
17 May 2022

bb0458df-a64b-4ad0-897f-080f80a6af7fR01